I0549281

Also by JA Sanborn

Karen Hunter Mystery Series
The Lost Cipher
The Orion Factor
Death Comes to Ely

All books above are available in Kindle edition or softcover at Amazon.com

The Stillwater Incident

Copyright © 2016 Dr. Jon A. Sanborn

All rights reserved. Except for use in any review, the reproduction or utilization of this work in whole or in part in any form by any electronic, mechanical or other means, now known or hereafter invented, including xerography, photocopying and recording, or in any information storage or retrieval system, is forbidden without the written permission of the publisher.

Swift River Publishing, LLC
P.O. Box 30965
Savannah, GA 31410
swiftriverpublishing.com
swiftriverpublishing@gmail.com

ISBN: 978-0-9968082-7-9

THE STILLWATER INCIDENT

The
Stillwater Incident

a novel
by
JA Sanborn

A Karen Hunter Mystery

This book is a work of fiction. All names, characters, organizations, events, and places in this novel are from the imagination of the author or are fictitiously used. Any similarities or resemblance to any persons, living, or dead, business establishments, events, or locales is entirely coincidental.

LXXI   The Rubaiyat by Omar Kayyam
The moving finger writes; and, having writ,
Moves on: nor all your Piety nor Wit
Shall lure it back to cancel half a Line,
Nor all your Tears wash out a Word of it.

Prologue

Stillwater Creek is located fourteen miles from City Hall in Middlefield running in a southwesterly direction where it intercepts the Oconee River, which adds its annual flow into the Ocmulgee River and thence into the Altamaha on its way to the Atlantic Ocean.

Residents today are unsure how Stillwater Creek came by its moniker, since those who might have known, have long since passed into the fog of the ages. Had local customs been maintained, though, Stillwater Creek should have always borne an Indian name. But the creek, with its slow and placid nature, may have simply enticed people to refer to it that way. In any event, map-makers enshrined their creations with the modern name.

Old Albany Road winds its way due west out of Middlefield where it crosses a narrow, stone bridge over Stillwater Creek on its determined pathway to the town of Lizella in Crawford County. Not much has changed since the rut defined trail was modernized back in the early thirties. The road surface is well worn representing a typical Georgia back road with barely two automobile lanes wide having no breakdown lane provisions; monotonously separated by a double yellow line; repainted every five years; restricting vehicles in the same lane from passing each other for miles on end.

Today, houses are sprinkled along both sides of the road separated by large, overgrown fields reminding those who pass by that they are seeing remnants of grand old farms. Over the years, farm acreage had been sold into building lots and homes have been constructed adding to the small population growth along Old Albany Road.

The original farm houses were not built in the style of plantation manors, but were more utilitarian. Houses started out small and as families grew, rooms were added to accommodate the new inhabitants, which resulted in undefinable architecture.

Most of the existing farm houses had been prudently maintained over the years, but a few had seen owners who had not sustained their heritage in the style of southern pride.

Many of the houses had been built in the years before the second world war and included for the time, modern conveniences such as running water and indoor lavatories. Most designs had multiple bedrooms and dining rooms instead of formal parlors.

Two of these homes had been built in 1954 and were the most recently constructed on the road. The first of the two was located on the Middlefield side of Stillwater Creek and bore the house number 1520.

It was in the second, lovely old house at 1522 Old Albany Road, located a short distance from Stillwater Bridge on the Lizella side that gruesome events occurred in the early Wednesday afternoon of July 18, 1979.

Chapter One

Marisa Delgado had begun dating John Forrester during his last year at Middlefield High. Marisa, better known to her friends as Mae, was a looker at a petite five foot-two, dark brown eyes and dark brown flowing hair that swept below her shoulders. She had a vivacious personality and developed many friends; never wanting for companions. In fact, some were close friends who remained as confidants well beyond her teen years.

One year older that Marisa, John was tall, barrel chested with a large head and somewhat horsey face. It had been a surprise to both his few and her many friends that he and the petite Marisa began dating. She had many male classmates interested in her, but for whatever reasons, she chose John. This was surprising to her friends because John was what everybody called "a loner" while she was one, about which classmates clustered.

Most of Marisa's friends could not understand what the pair had in common, but whatever it was, the two bonded enough to make serious life plans.

The two teens did not share similar family situations; Marisa had two siblings, a brother and a sister, much older than she; her parents having had her much later in their marriage. John had no siblings, which may have explained some of his stand-offish behavior.

Both Marisa and John had been taught a strong work ethic by their parents; they were above average in their school course grades and interests. Both were certain that they would step into a fulfilling life after Middlefield High.

They were typical teens with their Saturday night dates at the movies or dances. Of course, there was the late-night parking before going home. Sex had not entered the relationship, but both knew it would eventually happen if they were not careful.

On John's graduation night, it did happen causing a change in John's behavior toward Marisa. He now wanted them to marry before Marisa received her high school diploma. Marisa's parents were adamant that she needed to complete her education first. Marisa agreed with them. She had plans; she wanted a career.

Yes, she wanted to marry John someday, but not until she had completed her first step career-wise. Ricardo and Savanna Delgado could not afford to pay for a college education for Marisa. They both had worked menial jobs all their married life, but they wanted something better for Marisa. It saddened them that they could not help.

Marisa's career goals were sensible and not unreachable even without the financial help of her parents. Her plan was to find work after she graduated while attending Middlefield Junior College to earn her LPN degree. After that was done, she would work at the hospital, she hoped, and would work on her RN degree. As a Registered Nurse, she believed that she could play a vital part in the care and healing of people.

Later she would marry John if he still wanted her. The problem was that she did not share the second step of her career goal with him. Marisa knew that she wanted to earn a full nursing degree, but she did not relate that to John. She knew that he would not accept more education for her after marriage to him. She felt guilty knowing that her decision to withhold her goal from John was unfair. What she had no way of knowing was the impact it would ultimately have on their lives.

When John finished high school, he decided that college was not for him; instead choosing to immediately find work. His goal in life was to marry Marisa; buy a house and raise a family.

John learned quickly that what he desired and what he could afford depended on his ability to find suitable employment. He graduated with practically no saleable skills, and the only work available consisted of oil changes and washing cars with the Ford dealership.

Not to be deterred, John continued to pressure Marisa during her last year at Middlefield High to marry him upon graduation, but she refused. She insisted that she must finish her education to earn an LPN diploma. Both knew that it would take at least two years; until that was done, there could be no marriage; marriage and children would only complicate the road to that goal.

Additionally, Marisa had serious doubts that John could ever support a family on 'grease monkey' wages, as she called his employment at the dealership. Marisa pressured John to agree, although reluctantly on his part, to certain conditions for their continuing to be together after she graduated.

Aspiration considerations aside, Marisa was unsure if marriage to John was right for her or him. Worse, she began to have doubts about John's ability to provide for her and future children should they marry.

John continued to work his best charms trying to convince Marisa to marry him rather than waiting until she completed her studies. To forestall his push for early marriage, Marisa placed further conditions upon John.

Until he had a secure job, and more importantly to her, John had a solid position with a company, she would not marry him even when she graduated. Still, if John met her requirements, it would be a bittersweet agreement because her goal to become a Registered Nurse would have to wait, perhaps even to be given up entirely.

To please his future wife, John took night courses in business and engineering. He eventually accomplished step one of his commitment when he was hired by the Davis Arms Company located in Middlefield. There he was taught the skills of arms manufacturing starting on the semi-automatic handgun assembly line. John's skills and work ethic made him noticed by the upper management of the company. Within months, he was selected to begin a management training program.

By that time, Marisa had earned her LPN diploma, and John was on a fast track at work. Having met some of their life goals and requirements, Marisa and John wed in June of 1971.

In August of 1971, the house at 1522 Old Albany Road was put up for sale. This home was located within fifty yards of the west side of Stillwater Creek, just beyond the 'bridge' as locals described it. Even though the house had suffered flooding several times, it had been carefully restored each time by its owners. It was this dwelling, which the young Forrester' family quickly purchased.

By 1979, Marisa and John had been married for eight years; during that time, she had borne two children, a son, Daniel, age four and a daughter, Patsy, age two.

By this time, Davis Arms had promoted John to manager of their small arms line, and was being considered for the VP slot in the production department.

Marisa knew that John had old-fashioned ideas about marriage, but she hoped that over the years, compromises could be made to soften his position. After Daniel was born, John demanded that Marisa stop working at the hospital and stay home with the child. She had planned to take maternity leave and return to work, but that was not to be. Soon Patsy came along and Marisa was bound even tighter to the home.

John became increasingly adamant that Marisa give up a career in nursing. He demanded that she was to remain home; mothering the children until they finished high school. Marisa's aspirations conflicted with his idea of the perfect family tradition and her failure to tell John of her unbending career plans before her marriage to him would fester and come back to haunt them.

She was determined to work at the Middlefield General Hospital as soon as their children were old enough to be in school. This struggle lead to numerous arguments destroying the harmony they both desired and needed.

To keep family accord, Marisa maintained the home and cared for the children, but her goal of a full nursing degree and career was never far from her thoughts.

Marisa was a loving mother; often taking the children to McCrery Park in Middlefield to picnic and enjoy the outdoors. It seemed to be one of the few times a week that she could get out of the house. She longed for time to be with her own thoughts and activities, but for now, family duties did not permit it. As a wife, she met her family duties, but the constant grating of marriage problems caused her to enact revenge in the bedroom. Now neither John nor Marisa could discuss solutions in any meaningful way to solve their problems.

Marisa was an attractive woman nearing age twenty-nine. Petite, she had maintained her figure; shedding unwanted childbearing pounds after each pregnancy.

During their years of marriage, the Forresters had developed several friends who were always welcomed to their home. Several of these friends were women from Marisa's younger days with whom she could spend some of her valuable free time.

John had maintained none of his high school acquaintances. After marriage, he had developed a few friends who were coworkers at Davis Arms. One, Joe

Thomas, had sponsored him as a member of the Atlanta Shooting Club. As time went by, club obligations began to consume more of his time away from his family. Marisa was jealous and felt slighted by John's refusal to trim back his time spent away. The Club simply became another focus for arguments and outright clashes.

As the years progressed Marisa and John continued to bicker constantly about the unresolved issues that each had carried into the marriage. After a particularly dreadful argument, Marisa finally told John that she was going to return to school to earn her Registered Nursing degree. She tried to convince John that her goal of becoming an RN would be a blessing for the family's income. John demanded that Marisa give up her goal to continue her education.

Worse, John repeated his insistence that she not work outside "his" home, including any idea of returning to the Hospital as an LPN. This became such a sore point for the couple that terrible arguments developed into daily fare.

John's behavior was becoming more oppressive each week and he would often drive home from work for his lunch time break simply to check up on Marisa. It was during these noon-times that many arguments would start, escalating into near visceral fights.

Marisa dreaded those days and began to pack John lunches to encourage him to stay at work. It didn't succeed; John would toss the lunches or simply refuse to take them on his way out the door in the morning.

Marisa's complaints about her husband's increasing involvement with guns and the Club frightened Marisa to the point that she agonized over her own and her children's safety. The impact of these family hostilities had driven John to increasingly associate with club members to avoid the carping. The couple was in a serious stage of their marriage with no support to find ways out of the turmoil. They were at an impasse which was rapidly turning deadly. The only question was when the break would come.

* * *

It was on 18th of July, "a dog day," that the four-year-old boy had been awakened from his nap by a fierce, shouting argument. He pulled his pillow tightly over his head. He had witnessed arguments between people before, but this one was different, louder and more violent. His mother was yelling "Don't, Don't, Please." His sister was frightened and began to cry, so he brought her to his bed; cuddling her to quiet her down.

The voice was at once familiar, but in his shock he had doubts and was not sure he recognized who it was. He heard the front door slam and then a vehicle drive away.

Then he heard his father's voice strong and shouting. A few moments later, he heard another voice just before three ear-shattering explosions came from the living room. He began to wail along with his sister. The front door slammed; the house was now quiet.

Slowly, Daniel and his sister went into the living room and ran to their parents. Their small feet slipped on the bloody floor as they tried to hug their dead parents. Suddenly, a man whom both children knew came into the house. He picked up the boy and his sister; taking them to the front porch. The man then yelled to a woman on the bridge to call the police.

It was the Forrester's mailman whom the children knew. It was he who swept up the toddlers and carried them to the porch. According to the later police report, Robert Evans had had a package to deliver, which needed to be received with a signature. When no one answered the door bell, he opened the front door, as people often did in those times, and stepped in while calling out his presence.

Evans knew the family well, and knew that it was unusual for no one to be home at this time of day. As he stepped inside the front door, he noticed Marisa slumped on the sofa in the living room with John strewn back on the wing-back chair next to the sofa.

Evans could clearly see that they were dead. The two little children had come out from the bedroom; crying and slipping on the bloody mess; they tried to hug the only two people they had known who had loved them, but their parents did not move or comfort them.

Evans quickly took the distraught Daniel and Patsy outside to the porch. It was then he saw the Forrester's neighbor, Amanda Griswold, walking her dog and shouted for her to call the Police.

Within ten minutes, the first of several police vehicles and the ambulance arrived. The EMTs declared the two

Forresters dead, but removal of the bodies had to await the arrival of the coroner.

The subsequent post-mortems of the two victims resolved a few questions about how they had died, but posed many others, which had no immediate answers. The question of who had murdered the couple began a process that lingered on the crime books for many years. The police investigation performed under the direction of Detective Green of the Middlefield Police involved many man-hours and brought forth many more questions about the slayings than were answered. Of those questions and difficulties, very few were resolved until years later.

* * *

Marisa and John's children, Daniel and Patsy, were immediately placed into the State's Child Welfare System. It would turn out that their ordeal would not be over for many years. The loss of their parents and the inability of Marisa's or John's relatives to look after them required that they be placed in foster care. After being fostered for two long years, they were eventually adopted by a family in Middlefield.

The horror of what Daniel had witnessed tortured him well into his adulthood. The gentle dreams of childhood turned to nightmares where he was being pursued and killed. Both he and his sister, Patsy, were in counseling for several years, but it did not seem to help.

In the end, the psychiatrists thought it best to change the children's environment. And so after a time, the adopting couple and the Forrester children moved away to give them a fresh start.

Even with the complete change of environment, Daniel and less so, Patsy, were plagued by the fear that rode their backs until middle age when they decided to take action to get some closure of their parents' deaths by the only method they knew. It would take pressure from the Forrester children for the case to be re-activated.

Chapter Two

At the time of the murders, Detective Green, head of the Middlefield MCU, began an intense investigation to capture the killer of two of its citizens. Family members, friends, and associates of the Forresters were subjected to intense interviews for the remaining part of 1979 and work on the case continued well into the last months of 1990 before all active investigative effort was terminated.

At the time, Green felt that the person most likely involved in the killings was a handyman, Randy Williams, who was well acquainted with the Forresters and their property. His presence at their home on the day of the slayings coupled with an incident with Mrs. Forrester which had occurred a few weeks before the Forresters' deaths, convinced Detective Green that he knew who killed the couple.

Using details garnered by the MCU, Green's team believed that Williams had the motive, means, and opportunity to commit the crimes. However, after failing to develop indisputable evidence against him, the District Attorney advised Green to pursue other suspects and Williams was eventually excluded. Worse for Green and the MCU, the initial high hopes of solving the murders faded and their preliminary suspect list continually shrank until it simply didn't exist.

In fact, no one was ever arrested or tried for the twin murders, and the case went as cold as murder cases ever go. In 1991, the case was placed in an inactive file and the remaining part-time detective working the case was reassigned to other tasks.

With no statute of limitations on murder, thirty-four years after the murders, the Forrester children sent a letter to the Middlefield Police to reopen their parents' murder case and find the killer.

2341 Willard Street
San Jose, CA 95138

Dear Chief Tate,

I recently wrote to your Mayor Hampton concerning a horrible incident, which occurred in your city in 1979. He referred me to you, so that is the purpose of my writing to you.

In 1979, I, Daniel, was four years old and my sister, Patsy, was two. That was the year in which everything changed in our short lives. I have referred to what happened as an incident because my memory of it prevents me and Patsy from calling it what it was. Patsy says that she cannot remember much of that day, but I have some recollection even though it is distorted, I am sure.

Our Mother's maiden name was Marisa Delgado. We want to be certain that our Hispanic heritage does not flavor the investigation. We think you can understand that.

Sometime after the incident, both of us were adopted by a loving couple and grew to adulthood in

California. Patsy and I are now in our thirties and need to have some closure of that sad day.

Our parents were Marisa and John Forrester. Upon our adoption, our surname was changed, so we were known as Daniel and Patricia Martinez.

Our request is that you re-open the case file you have and provide any information that is available concerning the deaths of our biological parents. Even though they requested help from your Department, our adopting parents were not able to provide any information for us about that terrible day.

Over the years though, we have obtained smatterings of other information, which has led us to believe that you have information about who killed our parents. We have heard rumors that the murderer was protected for some reason. We don't want to accuse anyone if they are not guilty, but we want justice for our parents. We ask that you please reopen the case so that we and our families may have some peace.

Sincerely,

Daniel Martinez & Patricia Salazar

Two days after receiving the letter, Chief Tate spoke with Mayor Hampton about the case.

Mayor Hampton, at age fifty-one, was tall, trim and in good physical health. He had survived several re-election campaigns to remain mayor of Middlefield for the past ten years. The good citizens had elected him in 2006, two years before a devastating murder case labeled *The Lost Cipher* had shattered the peace of the city.

"Mayor, the Forrester case is one of our very old files. We currently have in storage the evidence, well, most of it I believe, which was collected at the time, as well as the case folders generated during the investigation. Since it was nearly thirty-four years ago, all our institutional memory of the search is gone; those still living who were involved have reached a level of senility. Others, such as Green, have passed on."

"Well, Chief, is there really anything that you can do after all these years? The Forrester kids are threatening to take this to major papers because they think there was a cover-up. It won't make us or the City very proud."

"There was no cover-up, I can assure you, Mayor. Much hard work went into it with no results. Green was a thorough and honest investigator. I can't make any promises, Mayor, but Major Hunter and I will review the files and see if anything worthwhile can be found. Our budget only covers current activity, so if costs…"

"Frankly, Chief, I don't want to spend another dime on a hopeless investigation, but I don't see any way around it. The City Council has been tight with money this year; I don't expect much support there, except that most members are up for re-election this year; the publicity threat may change some minds. We don't want any bad press to affect the tourist crowds. If the money becomes a problem, bring a proposal to me, but I'll let you defend it to the Council. Fair enough?"

"Thank you, Mayor, we will start as soon as possible."

* * *

In 2008, Mayor Hampton's political skills had led him to hire David Tate as Chief of Police, who in turn had reorganized the Middlefield PD along with the Major Crimes Unit after the disastrous tenure of the previous Chief.

Hampton's choice of Tate had proven to be a wise, practical, administrative choice. Chief Tate's subsequent decision to promote Detective Karen Hunter to lead the MCU had resulted in the solutions of three difficult murder cases. As Tate often said, Karen Hunter was "a Godsend" to the community.

The Middlefield Patriot, the local newspaper, dubbed the cases as *The Lost Cipher, The Orion Factor,* and *Death Comes to Ely.* Tate felt certain that Hunter and the MCU would not disappoint him or the Mayor in re-activating this cold case.

Karen's Major Crime Unit was much different from the one she had inherited and modified years earlier. Personnel, equipment, and forensic techniques had changed considerably.

Karen had hired a seasoned detective, Grace Carpenter, from the Atlanta MCU who was a critical force in the solving of the first major serial murder case of Karen's career. Captain Carpenter had been a key support for Karen during *The Lost Cipher* case, but was forced to leave the MCU after becoming romantically involved with Karen's husband. During her tenure, Grace had been a key contributor to the solution of many murder cases.

Captain Susan Ramos was also one of Karen's early hires and was still with the group. Susan had been Karen's right hand support; by her side during Karen's darkest days. She had taken over as Karen's confidant after Carpenter left.

Other detectives had left over the years for various reasons. Lieutenant Don Martinelli was indispensable to the MCU with his ability to solve coded messages left by the killer in *The Lost Cipher* case. The Georgia Bureau of Investigation had offered him a similar position in its ranks. It was with great reluctance that Karen had supported his move and wished him well.

She had fired one male detective, Richard King, for conduct unbecoming an officer with another MCU detective, Caroline Sprague, by sharing the true color of her hair with the Middlefield Police Department. Caroline was transferred to the Atlanta Police Force.

Caroline's replacement was a young female detective, Carol Morgan, who had been brutally killed while on duty. Her death helped the Team to solve a series of murders. For Karen, her ability as commander of the MCU reached its lowest ebb.

Karen then hired, Richard Burnham, a rather brash

detective to replace Robert King. Burnham, for personal reasons, had left a similar position in the Chicago police force. Karen found him to have excellent detective skills, but he was somewhat hard to control.

Lieutenant Richard Burnham held degrees in physics and had inherited wealth, but early in his tenure with the MCU had nearly driven Karen to terminate him because of his insistence that they be a couple. After he eventually married Susan Ramos' sister, Aretha, he settled down. Karen, as a wise administrator, supported development of a successor for her. It was clear to all that he welcomed the chance to replace Karen as head of the group someday.

The newest hire in the MCU core was a young aspiring detective who had experienced a horrendous automobile accident, which had left her partially paralyzed. Sarah Green was industrious, hardworking and had become an important part of the MCU's functions. Karen's decision to hire her had been well received, but Sarah had shown herself to be as valuable to the group as the others.

As for Karen, she would celebrate her forty-fourth birthday in two months. She maintained her weight of one hundred thirty-five pounds, which for her height of five foot eight inches presented an attractive figure. At her age, diet and a strong program of exercise was required to maintain her good shape. Karen's hair was showing the stress of managing the MCU; each morning she noticed strands of gray becoming more apparent.

"Hmm, I'm still not too bad looking, but then the

bathroom mirror lies. Look at myself in a store mirror and I hardly recognize myself," Karen thought.

Karen had wed David Robertson, a doctor at Middlefield Hospital, in June of last year fulfilling a long-held dream to settle down after a rocky marriage and untold pain. After such a very difficult personal life, Doctor Robertson provided the tenderness and love that she had searched for.

Reporting for work that morning, she was not surprised to see Chief Tate arrive at her office to discuss his meeting with Mayor Hampton.

"Good morning, Karen, the letter we received from the Martinez family has touched the Mayor's heart. For the good of the community, we need to put some resources to re-examine the Forrester murders.

"We haven't done much with that homicide case since I've been aboard; if for no other reason than our integrity, Karen, we need to slog through it. Their kids have brought up the rumors of a cover-up in the murders; we have to prove that is not the situation."

"That is a ridiculous accusation, Chief; Green was not an amateur and he certainly was an honest cop. I feel insulted by such talk."

"I agree, but we owe the Forrester kids and our reputation a sincere, careful review of the case; politics demands it; justice requires it."

"I know you are right, Chief, but it galls me to think that someone believes we would cover anything up in a murder investigation."

"I know. Have you any initial plans for approaching this?"

"I've already begun, Chief; I showed the letter to the MCU Team. Susan took the initiative and has proposed that we put the entire MCU on it for at least three weeks."

"Can we afford to do that in light of other things we have to accomplish?"

"For a short period of time, I think it is possible. If another situation should happen, we will pull resources as necessary. The first steps of the Forrester review will require dedication of the entire Team."

"Is there a reason why Susan is so interested in the case?"

"When she read the letter, I think the surname Delgado caught her eye; although at this point I am not certain why. I know that she is close to the Hispanic community," Karen answered.

"Okay, are you going to give her a lead role?"

"Yes, I've already asked her; she says that she would like to do it. You know that Susan is my strongest support officer. She knows her stuff; I depend on her."

"I am not going to micro-manage this investigation, but what will be your role?"

"I plan to be actively involved. I also plan to assign Richard to this case in a strong supporting role."

"How are you going to approach the work?"

"Susan suggested, and I agree, that we should inventory the physical evidence first. Then she, Richard, Sarah, and I will begin the slow reading of the original interrogation files; perhaps we will spot something useful, which may have been missed by Green.

"Until we can get all the facts sorted out, I believe this is the best way. If something else happens currently, of course, we will have to drop this work until time allows," Karen said.

"Fine, keep me up to date on any developments."

"You know I will, Chief."

"Unfortunately, I have a message from the Mayor, so after I leave you, I have to give him a call. As I said, I won't micro-manage you, Karen, but I have a feeling that Hampton will try to; I will stop that, if I can."

* * *

"Good afternoon, Mayor. What can I do for you?"

"I want to talk a bit more about the Forrester case."

"I thought we had already agreed to what I would do when we met this morning?"

"I want to be sure that you are putting the right people on the case. It could very well blow up in the papers."

"I will have the entire MCU working it for at least three weeks. After that, we will have resources working on it as required. I want to caution you that it may take months to solve this. I am confident that we can do it, but that doesn't mean it won't be a hard and long undertaking. If a serious crime occurs during that time, I must re-assign people to that. I want you to understand that."

"I understand, Chief, but we have to keep at least one

detective working the case; any political pressure will affect my chances in the Fall," Hampton directed.

"Mayor, we will keep the pushing on to solve this case, if possible," Chief Tate responded.

"I'll take that statement as a commitment to get this done."

"Mayor Hampton, you know that Karen, Susan, Sarah, and Richard are first class detectives. I'm sure we will have success in this case. I might add, as you know, that we have asked for additional resources, but we haven't had much success with the City Council. Perhaps you could re-visit our request at the next session," Tate pushed.

"I'll consider it, Chief; presently we don't have many surplus funds. We already supply the Department with more than we can afford; you'll have to make do for now. I must be going. Call me tomorrow; I will test the Council members this afternoon. If I don't succeed, I'll ask you to attend the next meeting and make your case with them."

"Thank you, Mayor, good luck!"

Chapter Three

"I'm sorry, Karen, Hampton has asked that we keep him updated on the Forrester case. Also, if we need some extra funds, he says that he will support us, but I will have to sell it to the Council. He says that this small City is already doing more for us than it can afford. We'll see how committed he is to solving this case."

"Good old Mayor Hampton, typical politician: 'I have your back,' sort of. Thanks, Chief, I need to get this rolling."

Later that morning, the MCU met to organize the work on the case.

"Karen, if you wouldn't mind, I would rather not have to review the autopsy reports," Susan said.

"I think the three of us have to review all of the evidence. What is the problem? You have never been squeamish before."

"I know; you aren't aware of this, but my family had ties to Marisa Forrester," Susan explained.

"What kind of ties, Susan?" Karen asked.

"Marisa and my mother, God rest both their souls, were close high-school friends. My mother and Marisa did not live near each other; it was the high-school that brought them together. Marisa grew up near the Stillwater house. Mom grew up on the other side of Middlefield."

"Were your mother and Marisa close friends after graduation?"

"My mother told me that the two women drifted apart socially, but they did remain in contact for a few years by cards and letters about their children, marriages, etc., but then even that stopped."

"Do you happen to have any of those letters or cards?" Karen asked.

"No, I've never seen any."

"Too bad, possibly they would have had something we could use in this investigation."

"Perhaps, but I doubt it."

"Did your Mom or Dad ever mention Marisa's murder?" Karen asked.

"Yes, but she didn't say too much about it. I think it grieved her very much. She never said it, but I think that she felt guilty for not staying close as a friend. Perhaps she could have helped in some way."

"I understand that, Susan, there have been times in my life when I missed opportunities to visit someone before they died," Karen sympathized. "How about your father?"

"My father and mother were divorced sometime after the Forrester murders. He moved away from the state sometime later. I really have had little contact over the years with him. My brother and I feel he loves us but it is from a distance."

"That's sad, Susan."

"There was something strange about this whole thing, though. Carlos and I were at Mom's bedside when she died. She was going through terrific pain with cancer and was

26

very weak. I was holding her hand when Carlos left the room for a bathroom break. She tightened her grip on my hand and said something that I didn't understand.

"She said, 'Evil lurks in an unsuspected heart. I can't prove it, but I think I know who killed my friend. It was not who rumors said it could be. The police didn't ask the right questions.'

"I asked her who she meant, but Carlos had returned to the room and she wouldn't reply. Later that evening, she lapsed into a coma and died the next night. Of course, I never got an answer to my question."

"Who do you think she meant?" Richard asked.

"I have absolutely no idea. I thought about it for some time after her death. Several months before my mother passed, she had given me an old, locked, metal box, which she said contained some things of hers that she valued.

"She thought the contents would be fun to look at when my children were older, pictures, cards, etc. She said there were some personal things that she did not want revealed while she was still alive. She made me promise that I not open it until five years after her death; why it had to be five years, I don't know. I hadn't given it much thought over the years, so I haven't been through the stuff.

"I guess it's now time; tonight, I will dig it out and take a look. Whatever is in the box may have no value to our case, but in any event, I don't remember where I put the key for it," Susan explained.

"Well, if you can't find it; bring the box in, and we can

try our luck at opening it," Richard offered.

"I'll keep that in mind, Richard."

"Richard, would you like to toss a coin to do a first review of the autopsy reports?" Karen offered.

"Why don't you take them? I would rather spend my time with the physical evidence."

"Well, again, we all have to review every part of the file documents and the physical evidence. I want fresh eyes looking for errors.

"On second thought, it might be better for me to review them first. I may have a question for Gordon, since he was the medical examiner back then. I will bet he has something to add."

"Have you had a chance to see what is in the evidence room, Richard?" Susan asked.

"I have," Richard answered, "It seems that Green and his investigators were conscientious in their collection of the evidence and preserving the chain of custody. The boxes and bags are all labeled and tape sealed with the detectives' names, dates, and initials."

"Well, that is one thing in our favor; we need to take out all the containers and place them in a secure work room," Karen ordered.

"I'm a bit worried about that, Karen, we need to be certain only we have entry to the room. If we are successful, I don't want some fancy lawyer questioning the chain of custody," Susan cautioned.

"I understand and I've taken care of that; I had the

keypad entry code changed to prevent just that. Only the four of us will have the access information. A sign is being posted so that others will know that room is off limits," Karen explained.

"Do you have any sense of anything specific that we will be looking for when we get to the paperwork, Karen?"

"Not really, Richard. The letter from the Forrester kids asks for resolution of the case; they offered a possible name, Williams, but that is only hearsay.

"Because of their age at the time, I wonder if Green's detectives talked to the boy; he was four then. Look for that in the reports; if they didn't, we should make it a point to interview them for any other information they might have gleaned up over the years. They may not like it, but they did open it up. In any event, whatever they say may not be of much value to us, but we can't take that chance."

"I think it is a waste of time talking to them. They were too young," Richard said.

"We'll see. Before we go to the evidence room, I want to say that I do feel somewhat uncomfortable parsing out the work this way. Trying to find things that may have been missed by earlier investigators is tough enough with one person focused to the task, but spread across four minds increases the risk of missing something, but I don't believe we have a choice," Karen worried.

"I'm getting discouraged about this and we haven't even started."

"Steady on, Susan, something will break; even with my

doubts, I have faith that with our talent, we will succeed," Karen tried to encourage.

"All right, let's get started with the physical stuff," Richard suggested.

All the Forester evidence containers held in boxes were brought to the secure work room. As each carton was opened, Sarah prepared a logbook of the container contents and their apparent condition. The current list of their findings was matched to the original inventory made by the earlier detectives; then each initialed the logbook entry.

Containers holding hair and blood were not opened by the MCU, but were visually examined to ensure that since their collection, the seals had not been broken.

"I believe that we have satisfied the transfer of the chain of custody to the four of us. Now we can categorize what we have. My hope is that this step will point us in a direction that will help," Karen said.

"I suggest that we decide which samples should be sent for forensic re-testing," Richard recommended.

"Good idea, Richard. Sarah, will you do the honors of scribe as we review the evidence?" Karen asked.

Sarah then wrote down the items on the flip sheets as Richard called out the items.

1. Crime scene photographs
    a. Living Room
        i.   Marisa Forrester on couch
        ii. John Forrester on couch
        iii. Much blood on wood floor

        iv.   Partial bloody shoe print
- b. Kitchen
  - i. Knife in found in the sink with John Forrester's bloody fingerprints on handle
  - ii. Blood spots on counter top
  - iii. Blood spots on linoleum floor
  - iv. Bloody shoe print
  - v. Smeared bloody fingerprints on the countertop
- c. Front and back entrances
  - i. Blood smears: inside front door
  - ii. Partial fingerprint on door jamb
  - iii. No evidence of break-in
  - iv. No blood evidence on back door
- d. Bedrooms
  - i. Master: no crime evidence
  - ii. Boy's bedroom: no crime evidence
  - iii. Girl's bedroom: no crime evidence
2. Small forensic samples taken at crime scene
   - a. Three hair fibers:
     - i. One was on the chair next to the couch
     - ii. One was found on Marisa's shoulder
     - iii. One was on the inside of Marisa's bra
     - iv. Test report in file: #1 binder
   - b. Hair samples taken of both victims
     - i. Test reports in file: #1 binder
   - c. Blood samples taken of Marisa
     - i. Test reports in file: #2 binder
     - ii. Typed as A
   - d. Blood samples taken from John

       i.   Test reports in file: #2 binder
      ii.   Typed as B
  e.   Blood samples taken from fetus
       i.   Test reports in file: #2 binder
      ii.   Typed as B

"That comes as a surprise to me, Susan said, "This is the first I heard of her being pregnant."

"There are probably many more surprises for us. It makes my visit to Gordon a must," Karen said. "Let's continue."

"Are these dried blood samples any good after all these years," Sarah asked.

"It depends, but I have heard that in many cases, forensic work can be done on them with good results," Richard answered.

"That is good news, but let's continue going through the items," Karen pushed.

  f.   Blood samples from the living room floor
       i.   Test reports in file: #2 binder
      ii.   Typed as A & B

"That makes sense; John was B and Marisa was A typed; I would expect that," Sarah interrupted.

"It certainly seems obvious, but someone killed them, so who did that?" Richard ventured.

"We need to keep that thought in mind as we slog through the rest of the case files," Karen mused. "One problem for us is understanding what actually happened that day."

"Well, maybe a seer could tell us," Richard sneered.

"We all know your feelings about that subject," Karen countered. "Perhaps that is what we do need to put us on the right track."

"I'll put my money on the evidence we have; let the ghost hunters live in their fantasy world," said Richard.

"Okay, we can agree to disagree and let the idea rest, but I again caution you that there may be some value there for us. In the meantime, let's move on," Karen ordered.

"All right, Karen, I'll let it rest."

    g.   Blood samples from Kitchen sink, & floor
          i.   Test reports in file: #2 binder
         ii.   Typed as A
    h.   Bloody fingerprint traces on the inside of the front door & doorknob
          i.   Too badly smeared: unusable
         ii.   Report in file: #3 binder
    i.   Bloody partial fingerprints from countertop
          i.   Test report in file: #3 binder
 3.   Shoe print analysis
    a.   Kitchen
          i.   Sole pattern traced to common sports shoe
         ii.   Test report in file: #3 binder
    b.   Living room
          i.   Badly smeared: unusable
         ii.   Test report in file: #3 binder
 4.   Bullet analysis
    a.   John Forrester

  i. One .22 caliber slug retrieved from his head.

  ii. One .22 caliber slug retrieved from his chest cavity

  iii. Both shots fired at close range

  iv. Stippling evident

  v. Test reports in file: #3 binder

 b. Marisa Forrester

  i. One .22 caliber slug retrieved

  ii. Fired close range to head

  iii. Multiple stab wounds to abdomen

  iv. Stabbing violence deemed overkill

  v. Location of wounds focused to the pregnancy

  vi. Test report in file: #3 binder

5. Clothing: Marisa Forrester

 a. White Blouse: blood stained

  i. Test report in file: #4 binder

 b. Tan Slacks: blood stained

  i. Test report in file: #4 binder

 c. Underwear: Bra/Panties

  i. Test reports in file: #4 binder

 d. Size 6 black loafer shoes: blood splatter

  i. Test report in file: #4 binder

6. Clothing: John Forrester

 a. Green work shirt: blood stained

  i. Test report in file: #5 binder

 b. Green Trousers: blood stained

  i. Test report in file: #5 binder

 c. Underwear: Tee shirt/boxer shorts

  i. Test reports in file: #5 binder

 d. Size 10 brown work shoes: steel toed: blood splatter

    i. Test report in file: #5 binder
 7. Vaginal swabs taken of Marisa
    a. Semen identified from a non-secretor
    b. John Forrester's semen tested-secretor
      i. Test reports in File: #6 binder
 8. Miscellaneous articles from crime scene
    a. No evidential value
    b. Separately boxed and labelled
    c. Reports in File: #6 binder

"Thank you, Sarah, your hand must be sore at this point."

"If I may say so, Karen, I think they did a respectable job at the crime scene," Susan offered.

"I agree; Green gave us quite a bit of information to work with…"

"But it didn't help him to solve the case, if I may finish your sentence," Richard interrupted.

"No, it didn't give him the answers he needed, but let's see if we can do better," Karen said with some distaste.

"Do we have funds to retest some of the physical evidence?" Sarah asked to change the subject.

"I'm not sure if any of the samples will need re-testing, but we should reserve that decision for later," Karen said.

"It is getting to be late in the day, may I suggest that we break until tomorrow?" Richard proposed.

"Tomorrow it is. I will contact Doctor Gordon and set a time to pick his brain about the Forrester' post-mortems. I would like you, Susan, to start reviewing the interview reports. Richard, focus on the test reports in the binders;

there may be something there that was missed back then," Karen instructed.

As the Team was leaving the room, Karen motioned to Susan.

"Susan, I am thinking of contacting Sloan Harrington to look at some of the physical evidence. What do you think about that?"

"Sloan did assist us on a couple of cases before, but this case happened so long ago, she probably won't be any help. The case is too old. Why do you think she will be able to assist us on this case?"

"Sloan told me one time that she has psychometric abilities."

"What did she mean by that?"

"She can touch items related to an event or person and develop a picture or have a sensation of events surrounding that item."

"So, you believe that we could use her talents by touching some of our physical evidence?"

"I do, but it isn't a guarantee. I know that Richard will be totally against it; I needed to know if you would feel the same."

"Call her; see what she has to say."

"Let's go to my office and call her. Be prepared for fireworks from you know who. I will let the Chief know what we are doing."

"Karen, do you realize that today is only a few days from the thirty-fourth anniversary to the day of the Forrester's murders?"

"I do, that is why I wanted to call Sloan; the timing might be beneficial."

"I don't understand why, Karen."

"Neither do I; we'll find out if Sloan agrees."

* * *

"Good afternoon, Sloan, this is Karen Hunter calling. Do you have a few minutes to talk?"

"I do; I had a feeling that you were going to call me. What can I do for you?"

"We have been tasked with a very old case, which Detective Green worked on some thirty years earlier."

"Whew, Karen, that is so long ago I'm not sure that I can be of any help."

"Would you be willing to come to Middlefield and try?"

"For you, Karen, yes."

"I think it would be important if you could be here on the 18th. Does that work for you?"

"I have a local commitment with my police department, but if I find it will run past the 18th I will let them know I need to break from them for a few days. Okay?"

"That is fine, Sloan, after thirty years, one more day or two may not matter, but I think the 18th is important for what I have in mind. Thank you.

"I have an idea or two about what I will ask you to do for us; if you can be here on the 17th, I will have a room reserved at the Inn and we can discuss the details when I see you. Okay?"

"That's fine, Karen, I'll see you on the 17th."

Karen and Susan lingered a few minutes after the call was done.

"I really hope that Sloan can give us some insight into this case," Karen declared.

"It is worth a try. I don't mean to be catty, Karen, but do you think she has changed much since we last saw her?"

"In what way, Susan?"

"Well, I wonder if she has put on some middle age weight. God knows that she doesn't need more in the chest department. The guys couldn't take their eyes off her last time she was here."

"I have stayed in touch with her by cards, etc.; she shared one time that her program of exercise and workouts have helped her to fight off weight gain. As you remember, she was a good-looking woman then who kept herself trim even considering the chest department."

"Goodnight, Karen, see you in the morning."

Chapter Four

"Good morning, Folks; Karen asked me to be here this morning because we have decided to enlist the aid of someone for this case who has worked with us in the past. I want you to welcome her; she may be able to assist us in the Forrester case.

"I know not everyone is overly fond of Sloan Harrington, but you must remember that she was instrumental in the solution of two previous cases. It will be a feather in our caps if we can break this case after so many years. She has committed to be here tomorrow morning," said Chief Tate trying to break the ice.

"Chief, I know that my feelings about psychics are negative, but I will do my best to make her feel at home," Richard said.

"Thank you, Richard, I expect nothing less."

"Chief, I have spoken to Karen about some requirements I have for the process with Sloan and she agrees," Richard said.

"What are the requirements?"

"We want Sloan to keep a journal of the events that day on official department stationary, so that we will have a written report when she leaves. My plan is to have it all video recorded. Also, we must direct her handling of the evidence," Richard answered.

"That sounds reasonable. Now I must leave and let you all get on with your meeting."

"Thank you, Chief," Karen exclaimed, "We will keep you updated."

After Tate left, Richard had an announcement for the group.

"Yesterday, I was curious about the blood evidence left on the inside of the front door and doorknob. In the evidence package for that item, it seemed to me that something was missing, so I opened the paper bag. The plastic sample envelope is not there!"

"Okay, Richard, just so we are on the same page; you have noted by date and initials the opening of the evidence bag, right?" Karen asked.

"I have; after I realized this, I went to the #3 binder and sure enough, there was a test report of that sample."

"Don't hold us in suspense, Richard, what did the report say was the blood type?" Karen pushed.

"The blood was typed as AB, which I believe is the blood type of the killer. That's only my opinion."

"Was that the only blood found on the inside of the front door?" Susan asked.

"As far as I can tell at this point, yes."

"The worst part of this finding is that we won't be able to do a DNA test if we ever identify the killer. That is a bad situation for us. Right now, it seems as though this is one of the slips, which Green's investigation may have made; not that we are proud to have spotted that," Karen declared.

"Yeah, of course back then, Green didn't have the luxury of DNA testing, so he may have felt it was not that important. He did, after all, have its type," Richard added.

"Of course, we don't know how the sample was lost or even, God forbid, someone removed it from the evidence kits. After we thoroughly review all the files of this case, it will be old-fashioned footwork to solve it, if we can," Karen cautioned.

"I would like to break for today and continue my work reviewing the binders," Richard suggested.

"Okay, let's meet at the same time tomorrow. Remember Sloan will be here," Karen said.

* * *

"Please welcome Sloan to our meeting," Karen said as she escorted Sloan into the meeting room.

Richard let out a muffled groan but controlled himself in front of the Chief.

Sloan Harrington was a tall, attractive woman in her late forties who had maintained her weight over the years. Her choice of a smart business suit enhanced her professional bearing and accentuated her well-endowed figure. Sloan had a pretty face, which presented a resemblance to a certain pixie look she must have had in her youth.

"I will let you all get to work," Tate said as he walked to the door.

"Sloan, you remember all the people here?"

"I certainly do, Karen; good morning to you all."

"Sloan, as I told you last evening, we have a thirty-four-year-old murder case to solve. You said that you were unaware of the Forrester murders; I believe that is a plus for what we are asking you to do."

"Thirty-four years ago, I did not have the developed skill I have today. I have no knowledge of the crime except for what you have related to me."

"Well, how do you think you can help us then?" Richard asked with a sneer in his voice.

"Karen said that you have no suspects and the original investigation also produced no suspects, so I may not be able to help you, Richard, but I need to tell you a little more about myself. When I was trying to convince you all of my bona fides in this psychic world, I told you the story of the little boy who I envisioned riding on his bike before he disappeared. I told you that I had the vision but could not tell who was his abductor.

"That wasn't entirely true. I did know immediately who the boy's killer was, but it didn't come from a feeling as I told you.

"I said that after a year, police discovered the boy's body buried in his basement and that the killer was his mother. All that is true except it wasn't a year later. I directed the police to his grave the same day I talked to them.

"You see; the boy's bike was found in the street; the police let me place my hands on the handle grips. At that moment, I saw the entire murder taking place. His mother was arrested that day and confessed."

"Why didn't that work for our cases," Richard pushed.

"Your physical evidence in those cases was practically non-existent, and I had had the feelings I described for you then."

"What can you do for us now, Sloan?" Susan asked.

"Let me answer that, Susan," Karen responded, "We have the three bullet slugs taken at the post-mortem and the bloody knife, which was used on Marisa. Sloan has told us that sometimes she can receive a vision related to an object by simply holding it, although it must actually touch her skin."

"So that means the knife cannot be in the plastic evidence bag?" Richard questioned.

"Yes, it does mean that usually," Sloan answered.

"Then I am concerned if we are able to arrest and try someone because of your chicanery..."

"Richard, that is enough. Sloan is our guest," Karen scolded.

Karen immediately regretted her embarrassing outburst; scolding was always reserved for private conversation.

"Karen, my concern is that some punk defense attorney will use Sloan's contamination of the evidence to get the killer off."

"I understand your concern, Richard; I have already spoken to our DA, Tom Hansen, and the State Attorney General about this potential problem. A possible solution is to have Sloan wear a sheer nitrile glove; if that does not work for her, both men agree that we should take the risk and let Sloan actually touch it.

"We will document and officially photograph the areas where she touches the knife and the slugs. That will have to be our defense should your trial scenario occur; I'm confident we would prevail," Karen explained.

"Sloan, does this method of yours really work?" Richard pushed.

"It does not always work, but many, many times, it does. If luck is with us here, I hope holding each of the bullets and the knife will help us to understand what happened that day."

"Are you bothered that the length of time, which has elapsed from the time of the murders, will affect your ability to 'see' anything?" Susan probed.

"I have to admit that it might. I have no way of knowing until I try it," Sloan replied.

"Are you saying that this whole effort may be a waste of time?" Richard asked.

"It could be, Richard, but we don't have too many options," Karen said. "I suggest that we move ahead with this process."

"There is one more aspect, which may help, Karen," Sloan suggested.

"What is that?" Karen asked.

"If it is possible, could I walk through the house where the murders occurred?"

"I can give the residents a call and request it. If they are willing, we will arrange to get you there. Let's move on with the plan to have you 'touch' the bullets and the knife," Karen suggested.

"I would like to have only one person in the room as I

handle each item," Sloan requested.

"Why only one person?" Richard asked.

"I need to have the room quiet. I cannot concentrate if there is noise. Also, the person will not be able to ask any questions."

"How will we know what you 'see' from each item?" Susan asked.

"What I will do is to hold each item and then write a detailed explanation of what I feel for each object. That document will be my official report," Sloan responded.

"Do you prefer a person to accompany you?"

"Yes, I would like Susan to be there if she is willing."

"Susan, are you game?" Karen probed.

"I would be happy to assist you, Sloan," Susan answered.

"Thank you, Susan. Give me a few minutes, Folks, I am going to try to schedule a visit for Sloan to the old Forrester house," Karen voiced, "Be right back."

Ten minutes later Karen returned to the conference room.

"Okay, Sloan, you are on for three this afternoon. Mrs. Johnson was a bit spooked by my request, but she approved our coming after calling her husband. In the meantime, why don't we break to let Sloan and Susan get to work?"

The day proceeded with the evidence handling and the visit to the old Forrester home concluding with Sloan's written report to Karen.

* * *

July 18th

Chief Tate of Middlefield Police has allowed me to attempt a psychic experiment to help solve a very old murder case. Captain Susan Ramos, of the Middlefield Police department has been appointed by Major Karen Hunter to observe and record my actions. I have been told that today is the thirty-fourth anniversary of the crime.

The experiment will consist of five events: my handling of four pieces of case evidence, and a visit to the house where the murders took place. I have not been informed of the history of any of the four objects.

Event Number 1:

I held the first object, a bullet slug, between my thumb and index finger of my right hand for five minutes. I immediately experienced a strong feeling that this bullet has an evil aura about it.

The hair on the back of my neck prickled as I have not often felt before. A genuine fear nearly overcame me, and a chill overwhelmed me with such strength that I almost released the bullet. This bullet was fired in a fit of rage. It was done to kill.

I then held the object in my left hand. I experienced no reaction at all. My belief is that the person who fired this bullet was right-handed. You must understand it is only a feeling.

Event Number 2:

As before, I held the slug between my thumb and index finger of my right hand for five minutes. The feeling I underwent was much different from the first. There was no sense of evil or fear on my part. It seems erroneous to write this, but it was as if this slug was meant to help, not hurt.

Holding the bullet in my left hand as before, there was no reaction at all. It's as if this bullet was used in a loving way, as strange as that may sound.

Event Number 3:

I treated the third slug as the first two. I had the same sensations as the first slug I touched. This bullet was fired in a fit of rage.

Event Number 4:

The fourth object is a knife described by Captain Ramos to be an ordinary fileting kind found in many household kitchens.

Using my left hand, I held the knife by grasping the hasp. There was no reaction, so I transferred it to my right hand.

I felt only a very weak sensation, which led me to believe that this knife had only a tangential role in this murder case. I believe that this is not the actual murder knife, but was handled by someone at the time of the murder.

Event Number 5:

Visit to the Forresters' home.

As Captain Ramos drove us to the house, I perceived a familiar sensation as we approached the Stillwater Bridge. The awareness of murder was very intense, but indefinite, in a way that was unfamiliar to me. As Captain Ramos parked the car in the Johnson driveway, the feeling subsided slightly.

As I stood in the driveway, a malevolent awareness came over me; a woman and man were quarreling about something, which I could not discern. The woman was weeping; then the sounds of two gunshots reached me. I looked at Captain Ramos; she did not hear what I did. We moved toward the house.

Walking to the porch landing, I sensed something malicious pervading the house. Passing through the doorway into the foyer, I felt a coldness, some vile spirit, which set my heart racing.

Suddenly, I felt something brush my left arm as it passed by. The sensation was electric; coursing through my entire body. It is as though my presence there has chased it from the house, but I could not be sure; the feeling of horror did not leave me. I sense that this evil specter has haunted the house from that terrible day. My mind is intensely aware of many things that Captain Ramos does not hear or see.

I continued walking into the living room, there were voices shouting, violent, angry, protestations for mercy, vehement accusations. I cannot quite hear the words of what is being said, but I sense the voices are male; when I start to move to my right toward the direction of the voices, they cease and all is quiet. Again I look at Captain Ramos for any sign that she is aware of the visions I have experienced. There is none.

As I resumed my walk through the living room, I heard a woman's voice screaming, pleading, crying; coming from my left side, but when I turned toward the voice, the screaming ended; then I heard a single voice; pathetic, begging for the pain to stop.

From the living room, I walked slowly to the kitchen, which was straight ahead. Entering the room, I saw water rushing out of the faucet, but when I looked at the faucet, it was shut off.

I saw a knife resting in the sink. It is unlike the knife I held at the Police Station. It is cruel looking; I know now that this is the knife used to stab Mrs. Forrester.

Suddenly, a hand reached into the sink and took the knife washed it clean of its noxious blood. It will not stay in the house. I looked for more communication from the spirits, but the visions and sounds have vanished.

At this point, I feel that I have perceived all that is possible for me. I have come to the scene of the murders; the house and its ghosts cannot or will not give up more. I cannot explain why some experiences of that terrible day have come to me whereas others have not. It is often possible for me to 'see and hear' clearly scenes of a murder. In this case, it did not happen. Perhaps the length of time since the murders has dulled my senses, or the house refuses to give up all of its secrets.

I am disappointed that I also cannot explain more of that horrible day. Perhaps if I had been able to go to the house on the anniversary of the murders, I may have been able to see faces and hear the words. When I explained this to Captain Ramos, she suggested that we return to the Police Station.

Signed this day: July 18, 2013
Sloan M. Harrington, Psychic
Witnessed: July 18, 2103
Susan D. Ramos, Captain, Middlefield PD

Karen met with Sloan after she returned to the station for further discussion. The conversation held only a few more bits of information based on Sloan's interpretation of what she had experienced, but Karen knew it would not provide enough to justify the expense of time and money. That was the risk and that was the result.

* * *

Karen was intrigued about the psychic's feeling of death at the Stillwater Bridge; but it only added to things not understood about the Forrester case.

It was two days later in the afternoon when Karen's phone rang.

"Karen, this is Sloan, I'm sorry to bother you again, but I had a very disturbing vision. It has bothered me since my visit to Middlefield; last evening as I was doing dishes, an overwhelming feeling of death happened again.

"I saw a man and woman in a dark room discussing something in strong terms. The man was insisting that the woman give him something the woman had, but she apparently could not find it. The man became demanding. Their conversation sounded as if they knew each other well, but they were not lovers. I saw a flash of light and then silence."

"Could you tell what they were actually saying?"

"No, I'm sorry. It was the tone of the voices which made me frightened. I wrote down a number which kept rushing through my head."

"Is it just a number or was there anything else that your senses caught?" Karen asked.

"There were other things which appeared; the only thing that sticks with me is the number 20," Sloan replied.

"That's not much to go on, Sloan; are you sure there is

nothing else?"

"I know, Karen, I am sorry it's not much help, but I wanted you to know."

"Well, thank you, Sloan, if you get any other visions, please call me."

Chapter Five

The next morning, the MCU convened to plan the day's activities and to review Sloan's events of her recent visit. After reading the notes Sloan had written, Karen opened the meeting for discussion.

"Before we get started, I have to tell you that Sloan called me yesterday to further explain a vision she had about her feeling of death when she was on Old Albany Road."

"Was it eye-opening?" Richard asked with his usual sneer.

"No, just more generalities; nothing we can use," Karen answered.

"Well, as I predicted, Harrington told us nothing we didn't already know and she may have gotten us into a pickle if we ever take someone to trial," Richard crowed.

"I must confess, Richard, it seems that you were right," Susan rejoined.

"I'm not as certain as you are that there isn't anything to be learned from her experience," Karen said.

"With due respect, Karen, you're trying to justify the waste of time bringing her here," Richard retorted.

"If she is right about what she thinks she saw and heard, then we can believe that John Forrester and a man were arguing before John was killed. Also, she hinted that Marisa Forrester seemed to be begging for the pain to stop. I ask you; if she was already dying, why was she then shot?

Additionally, Sloan senses that the knife we have as evidence is not the knife that stabbed Marisa," Karen countered.

"But it had Marisa's blood on it," Richard pushed, "So she must be wrong. How can we believe anything she says about this case?"

"It also may be that the person who shot them took the murder knife away with them, and planted another one," Susan responded to Richard.

"Why would they do that?" Richard snapped.

"Because, I think the knife, if it had been found by Green, could have been used to identify the killer," Karen responded.

"Sloan has thrown up a lot of 'ifs' for us to waste our time on," Richard said.

"I am confused about the running water in the sink," Susan said, "I don't see what that meant."

"No, and apparently, Sloan didn't either," Richard came back with.

"It probably means that the killer tried to wash the blood off something, perhaps the real knife used. Also, most likely, the murderer's hands were splattered with blood," Karen retorted.

"Okay, but of all the 'things' that she could see, why is that particularly important?" Richard snorted.

"Let me recap what I think she told us; then let's move on; we aren't getting anywhere by arguing about things we can't prove.

1) She believes that the knife we have is NOT the one used to stab Marisa.

2) She believes that the person using the gun was right-handed.

3) More importantly, she believes that there was another person besides the murderer in the room about the time the murders happened. I think that that hint is something we should not forget; it doesn't suggest anything solid for us to work today, but it may mean something in the future.

4) She believes that the woman's voice begging to stop the pain was a plea to end her life. Why? For that, Sloan had no answer," Karen explained.

"This whole episode of Sloan's 'visions' is still hocus-pocus to me; we've wasted our time," Richard pushed.

"Okay, Folks, we are done with her visit; let's move on. I sent you all an email late yesterday, which I hope you had time to review and think about.

"I was not able to schedule a meeting today with Doctor Gordon, so I wanted to pass an idea by you all. As I have said earlier; I am worried that the four of us working this cold case may cause us to inject our own ideas of what happened and why, and bias ourselves to miss something important," Karen clarified.

"What are you suggesting, Karen?" Susan probed.

"Well, I thought that each of us might try to create a scenario for what happened that day in the Stillwater house. Use what we know from Green's investigation and what Sloan has given us," Karen replied.

"Which is nothing, if I might say for the twelfth time. I see your reasoning, Karen, but how does that help?" Richard pushed back.

"I don't really know; let's try it; if this idea goes nowhere, we'll terminate it."

"We haven't had any time to review the reports yet, Karen, so what's the basis for our scenarios?" Susan asked.

"All right, I can see you all are not crazy about my idea, so let me give you my thoughts; reserve your ideas for another time," Karen responded.

"We're all ears, Karen," Susan said.

"First, I think that Detective Green did a superb job at the crime scene. I worked for Green a couple of years before he passed away. Do you remember him, Susan?"

"Not really, Karen, I was in the Department but not in the MCU at the time."

"He could be a curmudgeon to work with, but he was very thorough in his professional work. I think his professionalism shows by the physical evidence we reviewed the other day."

"I believe that is true, Karen, but can we get on with this; I am anxious to start reviewing the reports. We have thirteen large binders of reports and interviews to go through," Richard pushed.

"Okay, okay, I'll drop this approach for now, but I ask you to be thinking about your speculation when you go through the files. At some point, we have to develop a picture of what actually happened.

"If Detective Green made such a depiction of the killings, we can compare our thoughts to his. This crime is not so old that we can assume the killer has passed on to his reward.

"What I am trying to say, is that this role-playing work is worth our time. Let's break and reconvene in a week from now. I'll get a memo out with the meeting date."

* * *

The following day, Karen and Coroner James Gordon met at the morgue to review his post-mortem reports of Marisa and John Forrester.

"James, as I explained the other day, we have been requested to put manpower on the unsolved case of the Forrester's murders."

"I had heard; nothing is a secret around this place. I dug up the reports, photos, and my notes to refresh my memory. In fact, I still have my audio tapes made during the autopsies. It has been many years."

"Were you able to tell which of the two was killed first?"

"It was clear to me from their body temperatures that both had died at approximately the same time; well, they died within an hour of each other."

"When were you notified of their deaths?"

"Detective Green told me that he believed that they were attacked around one p.m.; I was notified by Green about two-fifteen. A neighbor had called the Police.

"This neighbor was walking her dog and the mailman screamed for her to call the Police. Apparently, he had a package Forresters needed to sign for, and he went into the house when they did not answer the doorbell," Gordon explained.

"They had two children, who were present at the time of the killings. We have a letter from them, which is why this case has been re-opened," Karen added.

"Yes, when the postman finally got there, the kids were crying terribly; he took them onto the porch. Apparently, the mailman was still trying to comfort them when Green's troops arrived. The children had run into the living room tracking through the bloody mess. When you review the photos, you will see that. I felt very sorry for those two tykes. I heard they were put in a foster home, eventually."

"You tried to talk to the children, I understand; were the children able to say what happened?"

"No, the girl was too young, and the boy so was traumatized that he couldn't talk. Green got nothing useable from him. I understand the boy went stone silent for almost two years afterwards.

"Green told me that both kids had been put down for naps or something, based on the mailman's statement. The timing seemed logical for naps; in any event, they apparently didn't see anything useful for us."

"James, from the autopsy report and photographs of the scene, John Forrester was not killed by knife wounds."

"You're correct; John Forrester received two gunshots. The one to the head was immediately fatal, but the killer also put a round into his chest. If the chest wound were the

58

only one, it might have been survivable, that is, if blood could have been staunched."

"What about Marisa?"

"Marisa was a different story. The killer did shoot her once; it was fatal, but I doubt that she would have survived her stabbings, anyway. The killer had taken a knife and stabbed her many times in the stomach.

"You know that the knife was taken from knife holder in the kitchen was found in the sink. Someone had tried to wash the blood off it, but I told Green at the time that I didn't believe that knife in the sink was the one used."

"What? That wasn't in the reports we've seen so far."

"In fairness to Detective Green, Karen, I told him it was my feeling only. The knife blade nearly matched the stab wounds, but there were some slight discrepancies; that is why I told him it could have been another knife."

"I know that this question is a bit unfair, but was there any evidence that Marisa was the primary target?"

"None that I am aware of; I don't have to tell you that her death was over-kill. If it were her husband who did it, his rage was uncontrolled. If it were someone else..."

"Yes, these types of murders are generally done by someone who knows the victim, but frenzy killings are also done by strangers triggered into a rage for some reason. That's another thought why this case is such a mess," Karen added.

"At the time, I thought it was the husband because of the execution style of his murder. Maybe a very bad argument that led to rage; I don't know.

"But then, who shot him? The shot to his head was delivered within two inches or so, as I could see by the powder burns. The one to the head was meant to deliver a message.

"I have always felt that whoever killed John believed that John was killing Marisa. If so, why did he shoot Marisa also?" Gordon responded.

"James, these questions are what made this case so difficult for Green and now for us. Someone must have been involved with Marisa; maybe involved is too strong a word, had been close to Marisa and killed John for what he did," Karen speculated.

"Possible, but who can say?"

"Did Detective Green offer any other thoughts to you about what may have happened?"

"Green told me at the time, that he felt Marisa was the primary victim; John may have unexpectedly come in just after the stabbing of Marisa. Why his bloody fingerprints were found on the knife if he hadn't stabbed Marisa puzzled Green and me, but …

"Over the years, I've come to believe that John Forrester was implicit in Marisa's death, but I have no proof; it's only a feeling. Who shot him and her, for that matter, obviously still remains a mystery."

"And he never found the gun that killed them. The murderer took it with him when he left. And your view that the knife we have as evidence may not be the stabbing knife leaves us without the murder weapons," Karen added.

"Right, that created a huge roadblock as far as Green was concerned."

"I should tell you that our psychic, Sloan Harrington, has the sense that you are correct; the knife we have was not used to stab Marisa," Karen said.

"You got her involved again?"

"Yes, and she has given us some insight into the happenings on the murder day."

"Well, I must admit she helped you a few cases ago."

"You had toxicological tests done. Was there any indication of drug use?"

"No, neither drugs nor alcohol for either one."

"Of course, no DNA tests were done on the blood," Karen added.

"Right, we've gotten used to that test in today's world. No, these murders occurred before effective studies were underway to accomplish DNA tests; reliable testing didn't really start until 1985. By that time this case had gone very cold."

"So, Detective Green never asked for DNA tests even when they became available?"

"Not that I am aware of; things got hectic in Middlefield; the city just didn't have the manpower to pursue the re-investigation."

"So now, it's in our laps. Can we review the blood typing that was done?"

"Yes, let me check the reports. Oh yes, Marisa had type

O positive; John had type B positive."

"When we went through the physical evidence recently, there were blood spots found in the kitchen as though someone had washed their hands and dripped blood on the countertop."

"Green thought at the time that he might solve the case from the blood spot evidence. It turned out that whoever left the spots on the countertop had AB positive blood; that is one of the rarer types."

"Right, but he was not able to find a suspect having that blood type. The other day, Richard found that a blood typing test report is in our files but the sample for that blood is missing. That sample seems to have come from the inside of the front door and was type AB positive."

"I can check later to see if I have a sample here."

"That would be great; we may need to have a DNA test done on it if we can ever identify a suspect. Were the children ever tested?" Karen asked.

"In fact, they were. Daniel had A type and Patricia had O type. Given the parents blood types, that would be expected, but not conclusive, you understand. An AB father could also have an A, B, AB, or O child depending on the mother's blood type."

"I understand; do you still have some of the Forresters' biological samples if we need more testing done?"

"I have some samples, but I'm not certain that they will be of any use, however, they have been kept on ice for all these years. Let me know what you need."

"At this point, I'm not sure we will need any; I'm just closing loops."

"Have you been able to review the police reports of the case?"

"The MCU crew is just starting to go through them; why do you ask?"

"One of the things that you must have found was Marisa Forrester was three months pregnant at the time of her murder."

"We certainly did. That fact was interesting, but the unanswered question is whether it had anything to do with the murders."

"Many, including myself, believed that it may have, but it was only speculation. That was my feeling back then, and I still believe that, but I wanted to be sure that you are aware of it. Green told me that since there was no way of knowing for sure, he let that idea drop."

"Well, DNA testing may put that idea to bed," Karen said.

"Well, there is still a chance that we can do some modern forensic testing."

"Thank you, James. Is there anything else I should know before I leave?"

"No, but give me a call if you need something."

* * *

"Good morning, Folks, I know that you've all been working hard on the Forrester case files. I've prepared a report of my visit to Doctor Gordon for you. I believe that

63

you all have received it. He answered many questions that I had, and I hope it will be useful for our work on this case."

"Karen, before we get started with the case files, I want to share what I found in the locked box my mother gave me."

"I hope you were able to find something useful," Karen said, hoping for any new clues.

"There were old pictures of me, Marisa, and our other friends. I had forgotten how beautiful Marisa was even at thirteen. There was an assortment of cards from Marisa and other friends of my mother; birthday, Christmas, Easter, etc. Other than numerous old family birthday cards, love notes from me and my brother, Ricardo, there was only a carefully saved letter in the original envelope."

"What about the letter?"

"It was from Marisa to my mother. It was written about two years after her marriage to John."

"Is the content something that you can you disclose to us?" Karen asked.

"The letter has a personal aspect to it; judge for yourself, but it is clear that after two years of marriage, things were not going as well as Marisa would have liked," Susan answered.

"It's unfortunate that there weren't any other letters or notes; it might have helped," Karen said.

"There is a trunk in my mother's attic, which my brother has. I have asked him to check it for any old letters, or any items of importance. I'll let you know if anything else turns up. Here is the letter for us to read," Susan said.

May 25, 1974

Dear Maria,

I wanted to write to you to let you know that after two years of trying, I am finally pregnant. We have been feeling that we would not be able to have children, but obviously, we were wrong.

The doctor says I should deliver in late October, but we shall see. Things are good with us, but John has been very short-tempered for the past year. Maybe I didn't go out with him long enough to see that side of him.

I am hoping that the baby will calm him down. I don't mean to say that he is bad to me, but just that it makes it hard to live with him sometimes.

I hope all is well with you and Ricardo. I heard from one of our classmates that you are pregnant too! You must write to me.

Love, Mae

"As Marisa indicated, my mother was pregnant with me at this time, so I'm quite sure that they sent notes back and forth, but this is the only letter I found in the box."

"Did your mom ever mention to you if Marisa had sent her any other letters that had a serious message?"

"No, I saw cards from Marisa and other friends," Susan answered, "If they wrote to each other on a regular basis, neither my brother or I were aware of them. So, I know that they exchanged cards and other short communications, but I never asked and she never said anything about letters."

"Well, that sounds like a dead end. Thank you for sharing it, Susan, it does give a perspective of John Forrester, for what it is worth."

"Yeah, Karen, I was hoping for a bit more to help us also."

"Okay, we need to move on. I'll save my Gordon review until later. Who wants to go first?"

Chapter Six

"I'll start. I reviewed the earliest interview reports by Detective Ron Callahan. I've put them in this draft form; I think it is easier to digest the data this way. First, I will list the two murder victims, and then the interviews," Richard began.

1. John Forrester, age 31, 1948-1979
   a. White male, 6'0", Blond hair, Blue eyes, 170 lbs., Medium frame, no identifying scars, moles, tattoos
   b. Had no surviving siblings
   c. Occupation: Gunsmith, Davis Arms Co.
   d. Father, Joseph Forrester, died when John was 12
   e. Mother, Katherine Forrester, housewife, age 67, in poor health. Interviewed by Detective Ron Callahan at Green's direction
2. Marisa Forrester, nee Delgado, age 29, 1950-1979
   a. Hispanic female, Brown hair, Brown eyes, 114 lbs., Small frame, No identifying moles, tattoos, abdominal scar from Caesarian delivery, last child
   b. Siblings: Ricardo, Jr. age 40, Miranda, age 21. Both interviewed by Detective Green
   c. Father, Ricardo, age 68. Interviewed by Detective Green
   d. Mother, Savanna, age 65. Interviewed by Detective Green

"Callahan's interview with Katherine Forrester, John's mother was not very productive; I'll read to you the rather short interview conversation. Callahan's side notes said that she was in very poor health with frequent wracking coughing fits and crying at the death of her family. Callahan taped his interview and later had it transcribed."

"Are the original tapes available?" Karen asked.

"I asked about them; it looks like they were taped over during the investigation."

"Too bad, false economy. Please continue, Richard," Karen said.

Callahan: Mrs. Forrester, do you suspect anyone who would want to hurt your son and daughter-in-law?

Mrs. Forrester: He was a good son. He never hurt anyone. He took good care of his family. I have no idea why someone would kill him. My friend, Gladys Goodson, loved him like a son.

Callahan: I would like to talk with Miss Goodson. Where does she live?

Mrs. Forrester: She lives down the road apiece from my son. It's Mrs. Goodson, Detective, Gladys Goodson.

"Callahan's side note for the interview was that 'down the road apiece' was at least a mile away towards Lizella," Richard added.

"What were the sites of the houses on Old Albany Road back then," Susan asked.

"Green had drawn a rough map of the houses on the road from Stillwater Creek to Lizella, and from the Creek back to Middlefield."

"Is Green's map in the records?" Karen probed.

"I couldn't find it, but he did describe it. There were two houses within two hundred feet on the Lizella side of the Forrester house.

Those two houses were razed over the years and replaced by 2001. The house the Forresters purchased was not and that is why they could purchase it so cheaply. There are quite several photographs of the three houses, at the time, all taken from the street," Richard explained.

"That concerns me; I hope we don't find that there are other missing pieces from the files. Green conducted a thorough investigation, so I am surprised about the map," Karen said.

"Maybe it will turn up. Shall I continue with Gladys Goodson's interview?"

"Yes, Richard."

Callahan: Mrs. Goodson, Katherine Forrester told me that you were close to Marisa and John Forrester, is that so?

Goodson: Yes, he was like a son to me. My husband and I couldn't have children so we sort of 'adopted' John. After he married, and moved to Albany Road, we were delighted.

Callahan: May I speak with your husband?

Goodson: I'm sorry, he is in a Lizella nursing home. He went bananas on me two years ago. He didn't even know who I was. You can talk to him, but you won't get much.

Callahan: I'm sorry, Mrs. Goodson. What can you tell me about Marisa and John?

Goodson: I didn't really like Marisa. She was too independent for my blood; she made him wait until she finished school before she married him. She could have married him out of high school and had her babies. Why she wanted to go to work, I'll never know. Two wonderful babies and she wants to leave them during the day. What kind of mother does that?

Callahan: Did John oppose the idea of her working?

Goodson: He did, he wanted her to stay home with the kids and be a good wife.

Callahan: Was she a good wife?

Goodson: I think she was, but I had heard rumors. I don't want to talk about them, though. I don't want to spread rumors.

Callahan: I think you need to tell me what you have heard and from whom.

Goodson: If I tell you, you must promise me that you won't tell anybody that you heard it from me.

Callahan: It will be our little secret.

Goodson: All right. I heard that a man we both know was very interested in her and she was not discouraging him.

Callahan: Is it somebody that I know?

Goodson: No, silly; somebody that John, Marisa, and I know.

Callahan: Well, who is it?

Goodson: He is a handyman who works in this area. He came to town about a year ago. He has done work for me and the Forresters. His name is Randy Williams, or so he says.

Callahan: Where can I find this Williams?

Goodson: I don't rightly know, but he is due to come to my house on Friday morning. Come back then. He is usually here by ten a.m.

Callahan: What kind of car does he drive?

Goodson: Early on, someone had been dropping him off here, but lately he arrives in a pickup truck.

Callahan: What color is it?

Goodson: It is green, I think a very dark green.

Callahan: Did you see the license tags?

Goodson: No, I never notice things like that. They were probably Georgia tags.

"Callahan ended the interview at this point and returned to Goodson's home that Friday," Richard explained.

Callahan: Mrs. Goodson, it is past eleven, is he usually on time?

Goodson: He always has been. I wanted him to clean out the garage today. It's such a mess; I want to park my car there.

Callahan: Can you describe Mr. Williams to me?

71

Goodson: He's about five feet eight inches tall. I only come up to his shoulders. He has a brown beard, not long but very full. He has a pony-tail.

Callahan: What are his eye and hair colors?

Goodson: I think his eyes are blue; his hair is dark brown. I don't know, but I am guessing that he is about forty years old.

Callahan: Has he ever done anything to make you fear when he is around?

Goodson: Only once and that was a while back. He was staring at me and had a funny look on his face. I asked him if he was feeling okay, and he said that sometimes he gets a strange feeling, but it passes quickly. I don't frighten easily, but that day I was nervous.

Callahan: Here is my card. If he comes around, or if you need assistance, call me.

"Before we break, Karen, I have some news," Sarah announced.

"What is it, Sarah?"

"I thought you might like to know that I found Detective Green's map of Old Albany Road. It was in a folder marked 'Notes' with nothing else in it. It was in one of the file cabinets in a corner of the evidence room.

"It is pretty rough; I don't know if there is anything to be learned from it, but we can feel better that records haven't been lost. Look!"

"Let's learn from this; please check all the file drawers for any more 'lost' items," Karen ordered, "Thank you, Sarah, finding the map makes me feel much better."

"You are welcome. The map shows the Larson and Wood homes. They were both demolished and rebuilt. We need to check the Middlefield Tax Maps for the current owners. Also, since the map was drawn, the opposite side of Old Albany Road has been developed in what Green then called woodland. I'll make a copy of Green's map and update it," Sarah offered.

"Thank you, Sarah, that's much appreciated," Karen responded.

"Callahan's notes indicate that Williams never came back to Goodson's house. A BOLO alert was distributed; they located him in Middlefield," Richard said.

"Well, when they questioned him, was he eliminated as a suspect?" Susan probed.

"It appears that Green couldn't find anything to hold him, but I haven't found the actual interview record, yet," Richard replied.

"If we want this investigation to be complete, we still must consider that he may have been involved," Susan said.

"I agree, Susan; anything else, Richard?" Karen asked.

"Only that Mrs. Goodson died in 1992; it appears that she had fallen and hit her head on the kitchen counter on the way down. There was a lot of blood as you can imagine. The mailman found her the next day. No post-mortem was done due to her age. Gordon viewed it as a tragic accident."

"I'm not sure the revised map will help us much," Richard said.

"It may not, Richard, but you never know," Karen replied.

I suggest we look at it anyway. I know it is crude and it may not help us at all, but Green thought it helped," Susan urged.

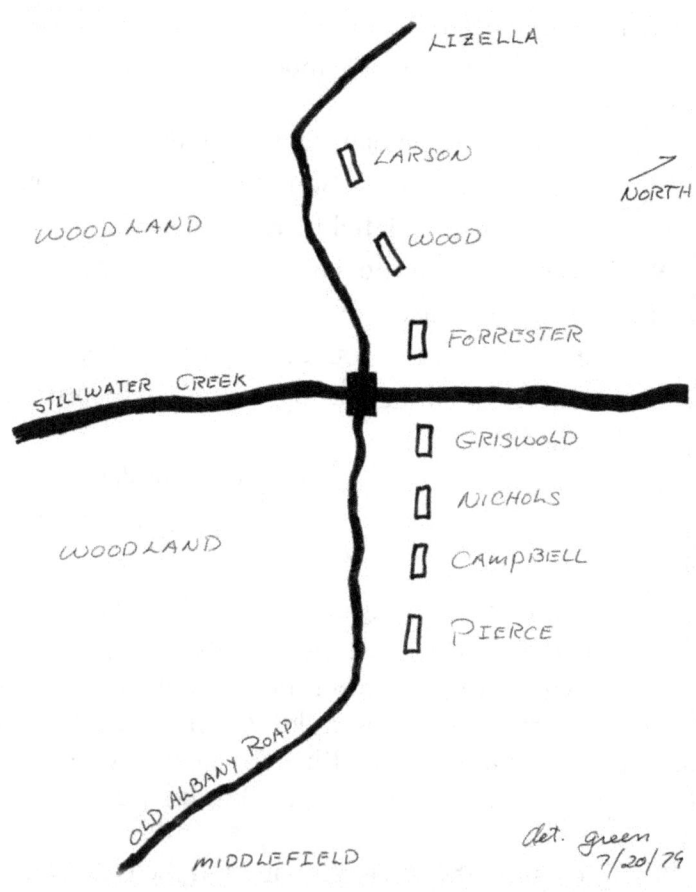

"Well, let it rest. I don't know how you all feel right now, but I am tired; I think we all may need a breather from this. Let's break until ten tomorrow morning. I have some things I need to get done," Karen suggested.

Chapter Seven

"Hi, Love, something smells great. What's cooking?" Karen asked as she walked in the door to her home.

"Roasted veggies. They should be done in a half hour. I stopped at Publix and bought two rib-eyes for the grill. Why don't you get out of those work clothes and relax? I'll pour a glass of our favorite wine before dinner," David suggested.

"David, you spoil me. I'll change and be right back," Karen said.

Karen had married David Robertson the previous June. The joy of coming home to David who loved and respected her was a fulfillment of her dreams. The pain of her divorce and loss of her child had not and never would be forgotten, but David had helped her gain back her stability and love of life.

David, in her eyes was an Adonis, a successful doctor at Middlefield General, a gentle and loving companion. A couple of years older than she, he was tall and handsome with his brown eyes and hair. For Karen and David, they felt that they could not have chosen better mates.

As the couple sat sipping their wine, Karen asked, "Love, how was your day?"

"My day is always predictable, although today it was apparent that Mr. Foster's pancreatic cancer is spreading much faster than I expected. I've made him and the family aware that he probably has less than a month to live."

"That's terrible, David, they are such a close family."

"We think we have such power over disease, but in reality, we have none. I am amazed that people put such faith in the profession."

"I think that their faith is so strong because you care, and that is clearly felt when a person faces the ultimate test."

"That must be it, but enough of my day. How was yours?"

"You know that I don't like to bring home what happens at the station, but I must admit this cold case we are working is very difficult. Going through the reports of thirty plus years back is mind numbing. I don't want to burden you with the details."

"You never told me about your visit with James Gordon."

"I know, I haven't talked about it for a reason; the murder scene was horrific, especially because their kids were there in the next room when it happened."

"I know that you've just started the work, but are any suspects popping up?"

"Not as yet, but we are hoping that something will trigger a clue. Enough of that, let's grill the steaks."

"Karen, you know that I am always here for you. If there is any way that I can help, please let me."

"Love, you know I will. You helped us with your perspective on the Orion case. The team still talks about it. Now, let's get those steaks going."

"Right, but I say that we should talk about the case. I am eager to help where I can."

"Okay, Love, I will tell you what I can. Right now, I am famished. After dinner, we can take some time, so I can get my thoughts in order."

After dinner, Karen began to reflect some concerns that she had about the case.

"David, from the case records, we know that Green and his MCU crew did the best investigation that they could at the time. In 1979, they didn't have the advantage of DNA testing, so blood typing was really the only way they could use to sort out who was involved in the stabbing of Mrs. Forrester."

"Do you have any actual blood samples still available?"

"Some, samples from the fetus, from both Forresters, and the blood smears in the kitchen were all saved. I will say that the coroner was very judicious in his handling of them."

"What did he do well?"

"He had samples desiccated and put in cold storage. He also had some wet samples sent to GBI where they have been stored in minus eighty freezers. Some of these samples will undergo PCR so we can do some testing. There is one glitch we have discovered so far, the blood sample from the inside of the front door is missing. At the time, it was tested and found to be a different blood type form all the other blood tested. We have that test report."

"Do you have any suspects today who can be compared to the preserved samples?"

"No, that is the worst part. Green had some men that he

suspected, but he couldn't get enough evidence to arrest any of them."

"So he and you both rule out that a woman couldn't have done the murders?"

"As of today, we don't believe that a woman killed the couple. We know that Marisa was pregnant, and Green at the time had no reason to suspect that her husband was not the father. You do bring up a point, though, what if Marisa was having an affair with one of the neighbors' husbands and the wife found out? Worse, what if Marisa's husband wasn't the father?"

"You told me before that Marisa was horribly stabbed and shot. The husband was only shot. That tells me that her murder was overkill; someone was teaching her a lesson, don't you think?"

"Yes, we considered that, but it is just speculation at this point. The blood typing tests done back then did not exclude John as the father, but someone else could have been the father of her baby.

"We will have a paternity test done if the samples are still viable. Even if John Forrester isn't the father, taking that information to the next logical step is nearly impossible. Time has worn useable clues to shreds."

"Gee, my job is so easy compared to yours. I hope the testing goes well for you."

"We'll see, I have faith we will find something, but that is probably my 'half-cup full' side talking."

After the dishes were done, David and Karen sat in the

living room as they usually did.

"Karen, do you remember before we were married, when we discussed if we had any pre-conditions for marriage?"

"I certainly do. We both had some. Why do you bring this up?"

"I had one from my early years, a dream really. I made a vow to give help to people who truly needed my skills when I became a doctor."

"Oh? And what was that dream?"

"Karen, I wanted to wait for a time when you were less stressed, but my dream was to do volunteer work."

"Do you mean to give up your position at Middlefield?"

"No, but perhaps to take some sort of leave to fulfill that dream. We can afford to lose my salary for a while."

"I think that would be a great idea, David. There are plenty of needy people you would be able to help."

"Actually, my thought would be to do a four-month stint in Arizona at one of the Indian Reservations. It would mean that we would be apart for that time. I could get home now and then, but not every week."

"David, why would you want to leave me and our new life? We just got married last June."

"I feel I want to help people who don't have the opportunities folks around here have. It would mean a lot to me."

"You know, David, that I love you so much; I would not try stop you. I will enjoy hearing about your work."

"I haven't told you everything, Love, it could be a commitment for one year in four-month portions. How would you feel about that?"

"I married you for all situations. If this is something that you feel you need to do, then I am all for it. It was only my petty selfishness coming out. I love you and I will be here for your return; you know that. When would you leave?"

"I would have to give notice at the hospital to take a year's leave of absence."

"Will it be for an entire year?"

"It will, but I get a week home between each four-month commitment."

"Is there any stipend at all?"

"Very little; just enough to cover food and gasoline. Medicines and equipment are provided by the government."

"That is okay, Love, we can make it on my salary and our savings."

"I know why I love you so much, Karen.

Chapter Eight

"Good morning, I've been considering the idea that we should have someone travel to see the Forrester kids. Even though they were very small at the time, they may have some residual memories, which may help us. What do you think?"

"Karen, you don't really believe that those kids will have anything to offer, especially after all this time?" Richard pushed.

"Richard, actually, I do. I believe that kids do have memories, vague though they may be, but they have them. Also, they were told certain things as they grew up about that day. I am sure some of it accurate and some of it not, but who knows without talking to them," Karen responded with some irritation in her voice.

"I agree with Karen. When I was about Patsy Forrester's age, I have a vision of sitting in a screened-in porch with my mother and grandmother talking in low tones. It was cool on the porch and I was playing with a toy while I strained to hear what they were saying. I think Karen is right in suggesting that we at least explore the idea," Susan voiced.

"Do you think the Chief will go along with the expense?" Richard pushed.

"I've already spoken to him. I think that we all agree it is a long shot, but the pressure is on to solve this, so yes, we should do it."

"Well, who is the anointed one to make this futile trip?" Richard pushed again.

"I was thinking that you are the ideal person for this venture. Are you game?"

"If you insist, Karen, I'll go, but I want to take Aretha with me. She's never been to the 'People's Republic of California.' "

"I knew that you would make that a condition. Chief and I are okay with that, but you pay her freight for the trip. Agreed?"

"Agreed."

Richard Burnham and Aretha Martinez, Susan's sister, had married last July. Aretha held an emergency room nursing position at Middlefield General, and worked with her brother-in-law, Carlos Ramos, Susan's husband at the same hospital.

"Sarah, please make the flight arrangements for Richard."

"I'll get it done. When do you want to leave, Richard?"

"Get us on an early flight on Monday," Richard requested.

"Very good. In the meantime, Susan, would you give us an update on Green's interviews?"

"Before I do that, do you remember that I said my brother had my mother's trunk of stuff in his attic? Well, he opened it as I asked, and he found more letters between my mother and Marisa Forrester."

"Are they important to us?" Karen asked.

"There were five letters; four of them were just chit-chat, but the last one, dated two days before Marisa's murder, was intriguing. In fact, my mother wrote a note on it because, I think, she was very concerned for her friend. It is very clear that Marisa was writing some sort of confession to my mother. Let me read the letter to you."

Dear Maria,

I don't know where to turn, so I am asking you, my best friend, to help me. As you know, John is a very jealous man. He told me to fire Randy, but I haven't done it. Randy did something he shouldn't have, but when I told John about it he nearly killed me.

Please do not judge me; I must confess that I became infatuated with a man. I will call him Prince. He has visited me for the past several months on nights when John is at his Club in Atlanta. I was the one who started it. I was stupid to get involved, but now I am in trouble; you know what I mean... I am so afraid and ashamed. I have to tell John soon.

I opened a mail box at the post office so Prince and I could write to each other. I burn all his letters and he said that he burns all of mine. I wish I really believed that. One time he had a letter of mine still in his pocket. What if his wife found it? I feel like such a fool. The other night I found a love note in his coat pocket from, of all people, Alicia. It was a strange note, but when I asked him about it, he said it was nothing for me to be concerned about.

I feel that he has been cheating on me. I'm sure that you're asking yourself how I can write this with a straight face after what I've just written about having taken a lover.

Last month, I started getting threatening letters coming to the house. They are from this woman, Alicia, and she says that she will make my life miserable if I don't stop seeing him. I believe that she will tell John. I don't know what to do. I have put her letters in a cubby in my desk. I would like to give them to somebody I can trust.

If John ever sees one of them or one from Prince, I swear that he will kill me. He has said that many times.

They, uh oh, John is coming in the door. I will mail this to you this afternoon. I will write again. Pray for me.

Love, Mae

"Let me read my mother's side note," Susan said.

I've told you before to call the police when he threatens you; you have been so foolish, Mae; who is Alicia? I will find out.

"Do you know if your Mother ever found out?" Richard asked.

85

"I think that was the message she was trying to give me on her death bed. As I said, however, I have no idea who Prince or Alicia are."

"Thank you, Susan. From the blood typing, we know that it is possible the baby that she was carrying may or may not have been John's. The letter confirms that John Forrester was brutish to Marisa and that she did cheat on him. That may have been the trigger for him killing her, but the question of who killed John becomes exasperating. The letter really doesn't help much beyond that," Karen reflected.

"There was nothing else in the chit-chat letters between your Mom and Marisa?" Richard asked.

"I'll make copies for you, but no; they were written before Marisa's indiscretion; they're just two people exchanging news of their families."

"Well, let's continue with our process. Susan, what about Green's interview reports?"

"Green interviewed Marisa's parents and siblings. Can I put up quick bios of them?"

"Certainly, Susan, it helps," Karen answered.

"Then I'll follow Richard's lead."

1. Ricardo Delgado, age 68, hardware store owner
2. Savanna Delgado, nee Espinoza, age 65, housewife
3. Ricardo Delgado, Jr., age 40, Electronic salesman

4.   Miranda Delgado, age 21, student at Georgia
     State

Green: Thank you Mr. Delgado, I appreciate your willingness to talk to me so soon after this tragedy. I know it is difficult, but the more information we can gather now will help us to solve your daughter's murder.

Ricardo: I want to help, but I'm not sure what I can do to assist you.

"Green's side note was that Ricardo cried whenever Marisa's name was mentioned," Susan interjected.

Green: Do you have any idea why someone would want to harm Marisa?

Ricardo: Marisa was so loving and gentle. I don't know why anyone would want to kill her.

Green: Did she ever mention any of her friends?

Ricardo: She had a few friends from high school and college. She often spoke of Maria Martinez and other girlfriends, but I don't think she was close to any of them.

Green: Did she ever mention anyone who gave her any trouble?

Ricardo: She did tell me a month back that a man who did some work for them around the house gave

87

her a funny feeling. She couldn't explain the feeling; she said it wasn't fear, but his presence bothered her, so they decided to not hire him anymore.

Green: Was there any trouble when they let him go?

Ricardo: My gutless son-in-law told me that this man threatened to burn their house down.

Green: Who was the man?

Ricardo: They never told me his name.

Green: Why didn't you or they call the police?

Ricardo: The police never come out this way because we are Hispanic.

Green: Oh, please, Ricardo, John Forrester wasn't Hispanic and further, my mother was Hispanic. I don't know where you got this idea, but it's wrong. We answer all calls.

Ricardo: It is my family's experience.

Green: Ricardo, this is not helping. Did they describe the man to you?

Ricardo: No, never.

Green: Is there anything else you can tell me about your daughter and son-in-law?

Ricardo: No, except that I told her not to marry him, but she did it out of spite.

Green: Thank you, Ricardo. You've been a help.

Ricardo: Please find out who killed my beautiful Marisa.

Green: We will do all that we can. Trust us.

"I should add here that Green's side note indicates that Ricardo was not that helpful, as you can see, and that he felt Ricardo was hiding something," Susan added.

"Maybe we'll eventually find out what he was hiding, but let's move on," Karen advised.

"Okay, the next interview was with Marisa's mother."

Green: Mrs. Delgado, thank you for speaking with me. I know how heartbreaking it must be for you, but the sooner we can get information, the better are our chances to find the killer of your daughter and son-in-law.

Mrs. Delgado: Detective, please call me Savanna. I will do what I can to help you find Marisa's killer.

Green: Savanna is such a pretty name; it was my mother's name.

Savanna: I don't care about finding his killer.

Green: You don't care about John Forrester?

Savanna: He made Marisa's life miserable. He was not nice to her. Sometimes she would have bruises on her arms. I always knew he hit her when she wore blusas manga to hide her shame. I told her not to marry him.

Green: What else can you tell me about Forrester?

Savanna: He harassed her all the time her about

her wanting to work. All the money we spent to get her nursing degree and he wouldn't let her use it. He was an evil man, Detective.

Green: Why didn't she get a divorce?

Savanna: We are Catholic. We don't divorce; we suffer in silence.

Green: I am Catholic also, but it would not stop me from getting a divorce if it meant less pain for my children. My sister was divorced from her husband after five years and two children. I think that she did the right thing.

Savanna: Marisa told me that he threatened to kill her if she walked out on him. She said that he was insanely jealous.

Green: I hate asking this question, Savanna, but did Marisa ever have a lover?

Savanna: She did not ever say that, and I don't believe it, but I could tell something had changed in her. I know that she was a faithful wife. She said that she and that pig she was married to were getting along better. I didn't really believe that; he was so terrible to her. But, Detective, if she did stray, I can't imagine how she managed that.

Green: What about Forrester? Was he faithful to Marisa?

Savanna: Marisa was sure that he did have women he visited.

Green: Did she give you any of their names?

Savanna: Recently, I picked her and the children up. We were at my home, and we had a chance to talk. She was deeply depressed that day. When I asked her what was bothering her, she said she knew that John was cheating on her. She suspected it was one of three women he was seeing. Marybeth Taylor and Constance Lewis.

Green: Who was the third person?

Savanna: My daughter, Miranda, came into the room just then; Marisa clammed up, and so I never learned the third name.

Green: Would you have any way of finding out who the third person is?

Savanna: I can't help there; I wouldn't know. She said that she was reaching her limit; she would take the children and walk out on John even with his threats to kill her.

Green: Was there anything else you can say about her that day you two spoke?

Savanna: She told me that she was pregnant and couldn't bear the thought of having another of Forrester's babies.

Green: I hesitated to ask you about it, but the Medical Examiner did find that Marisa was pregnant. I'm glad she told you.

Savanna: Detective, why did the killer stab her so

much?

Green: I can't say for certain, but it appears that Marisa was the intended target because of the violence. John Forrester may just have been in the wrong place at the wrong time.

Savanna: I wish the killer had been after him.

Green: Well, we don't know for sure, if she was the target, but we will find Marisa's murderer, Savanna. Thank you, I know this has been a terrible strain on you and your family.

Savanna: My prayers are with you, Detective. Bring this killer to justice. I hope he tries to escape and you kill him.

"On that sour note, Green ended the interview," Susan said.

"There is something I can't quite understand, Susan. Did Green have anything in the notes about why Marisa's parents did not take the Forrester children to raise?" Karen asked.

"No, he only mentions it as a passing thought. Neither John Forrester's mother or the Delgado's family agreed to take them. My belief is that they were too old to take on a two and four-year-old."

"Sarah, would you see if we can get a look at the court adoption records. Since they are usually sealed, it may take some time to get a release. Of course, this was not a usual case; it was not a secret who the parents of the children and the adoptive family were, so perhaps, the records are not sealed," Karen speculated.

"In the meantime, should we continue with Marisa's two siblings' interviews? They are relatively short," Susan offered.

"It's getting late, but let's finish up the Delgados," Karen said.

"The first is her brother, Ricardo. As I said earlier, Detective Green interviewed all of them."

Green: Mr. Delgado, thank you for taking time to talk with us. The sooner we have any useable information; the sooner we can catch your sister's killer.

Ricardo, Jr: Please call me Rico. It's the nickname I grew up with. I appreciate that; how can I help?

Green: Were you and Marisa close as siblings?

Rico: I'm eleven years older than Marisa, so I was long gone as she went into her teen years. Miranda and Marisa were eight years apart. They may have had similar friends and experiences.

Green: What do you do for a living?

Rico: I'm an electrical engineer. I work in Silicon Valley and live in Mountain View. It's a beautiful city.

Green: Do you travel back to the family very often?

Rico: Only for Christmas. My wife is also an engineer and finding time to take vacations is difficult; you know, working for different companies has its problems.

Green: When you were last home for Christmas, did Marisa share any confidences with you?

Rico: Funny thing, we went for a walk together and as we made our way onto the Stillwater Bridge, she said something that seemed out of place for her. She said, "Rico, if something ever happens to me, promise me that you will talk to my friend, Luz. I have sent her information, which she will share with you."

Green: Did she give you any idea why she was thinking about something happening to her?

Rico: I do know from my mother that she and John were having problems, but I didn't ask her. Actually, I was too stunned to question her about it.

Green: Do you know who this Luz is?

Rico: I have no idea who Luz is and I am sorry now that I didn't ask her at the time. I asked my family last night about her, but they don't know either. The most they could offer was it might be an old high school friend.

Green: We need to find her. Did anyone in the family have an idea about locating her?

Rico: None.

"With that, Green closed the interview and wrote a side

note: 'So far, the family is genuinely trying to help. Marisa, unfortunately, did not leave enough of a trail for us to follow.' "

"That only leaves one direct family member, Miranda, to cover for today, right, Susan?" Karen asked.

"Yes, here goes."

Green: Miranda, you know that we have been talking to all your family members about Marisa. I want to thank you for agreeing to spend time with me under these difficult circumstances.

Miranda: Please call me Mia, everyone does.

Green: Okay, Mia, I know that Rico asked you all about this person, Luz. Is there anything that you can tell me that I could use to find her?

Mia: I can't think of anyway to identify her. Rico told us what Marisa had said to him. It seems that she had an idea that someone was going to hurt her, but...

Green: Did Marisa ever share any confidences with you?

Mia: No, not really.

Green: Is there anything you know that could help us to solve Marisa's murder?

Mia: I'm sorry, but I can't think of anything.

"With that, the interview was over," Susan concluded.

"I believe that I've had enough for today. Richard, please get ready for your trip. We will reconvene when you return," Karen instructed.

"Richard, I have your tickets on Delta at seven next Monday morning to San Francisco for Daniel's interview. I've given you two days before you fly down to San Diego for your interview with Patricia. I hope that is enough time to see the sights," Sarah announced.

"That sounds okay, Sarah. We'll spend more time in San Diego; the sights are better," Richard responded.

Chapter Nine

"Welcome back, Richard, we are all anxious to hear about your travels. Did Aretha like the sights?" Karen asked.

"Yes, it was her first time to San Francisco. Of course, we had to fly down to San Diego where Patsy is located. Her husband is a Lieutenant in the Navy and stationed there."

"Well, what have you found out?"

"As I said before I left, I didn't think it was worth the expense to fly out there. I have typed up my report for the files."

"We will all read it as time permits, but it would be good if you could explain some things so we can do some give and take."

"Okay, here goes. After all these years, Patsy does not have much memory of that day; she was, after all, only two years old. She did say that she had vague memories of people coming to her house many times. People picked her up and played with her, but that was only an impression. She felt sure that it wasn't her la abuela because she knew her."

"So she knew it wasn't her Grandmother picking her up," Susan said.

"Right, I had to ask her what she meant by that. Other than that, she really didn't have much to offer. She did tell me that over the years her adopted parents had told her that whoever killed her mother and father was not a stranger to them," Richard continued.

"That makes sense from the evidence found at the house. Whoever it was, was welcomed into the home by the Forresters. There was no forced entry," Susan added.

"Before we go any further with this line of reasoning, perhaps you should relate what Daniel had to say, Richard," Karen directed.

"Yes, if anything made the trip worthwhile, it was what Daniel had to say. He said that the memory was really a blur, but with his adopted parents help, he was able to somehow put his memories behind him. He had terrible nightmares of the day. Both he and his sister went through counseling as they got older.

"He told me, as best he can recollect, that on that day, his mother had put them down for a nap as usual. That happened every day about one o'clock when his father came generally home for lunch. He had just gotten off to sleep when he heard someone ring the doorbell.

"Then he heard angry voices. He heard his mother's voice, but there was a voice he didn't recognize. Although he could hear the shouting, he didn't understand what they were saying. He heard strange noises; he heard his mother yelling 'no, no, no,' and then it was quiet. Afterwards he heard the front door slam.

"The next thing he remembered was his father and someone shouting at each other. That was odd, because his parents sometimes had arguments when his father came home for lunch, but this time was different. There were two loud bangs and then another one a few minutes later.

"He said he was scared; stayed in his room until it was quiet again; then he and Patsy came running out and saw their parents. They ran to their mother and father and hugged them; their clothes became soaked with their parents' blood.

"Daniel said that the postman came to the door; saw what had happened; picked him and his sister up and took them to the porch. He thinks it was the postman who called the police. Daniel said he remembered the postman because he often came to the house and talked to his mother when he was delivering mail."

"Your intuition was correct, Richard, it wasn't worth the trip. The only thing that Daniel confirmed was that someone had an argument with his parents and killed them, but we already knew that. I'll tell the Chief and take the heat," Karen said.

"Well, there was one thing that Daniel told me that got me thinking about the letter Susan gave to us," Richard added.

"What was that?" Susan asked.

"He said that he remembers telling his father that sometimes a man came to talk with his mother. He thinks he told him sometime before the day his parents were killed, but he couldn't say for sure. Maybe his memory was failing. He did remember that when he told his father, a huge fight happened between his parents."

"That's interesting, but I don't know what to do with it. We already know that John was very jealous," Karen replied.

"Well, that was all I got out of them. Anything important happen while I was gone?" Richard asked.

"Sarah read several of Detective Foster's interviews, but we haven't discussed them yet. I think this is a good time to review them since you're back. Are you ready, Sarah?" Karen asked.

"I am; the first interview I'll talk about is the one with the postman, Robert Evans; he was the person who discovered the bodies that afternoon. I'll read what Detective Foster wrote."

Foster: Thank you for talking to me today. I know that you are very upset, but we have to get this done.

Mr. Evans: I understand, but it is very difficult. The Forresters were good friends. I can't believe anyone would want to hurt them in such a brutal way.

Foster: Mr. Evans, what time did you discover the scene at the Forrester home?

Mr. Evans: It was about one-forty-five or closer to two o'clock. I can't be sure of the time, because it unnerved me so much today.

Foster: What time do you usually get to the Forrester home on your delivery route?

Mr. Evans: Generally, it is between 11:30 and

quarter to noon. Today I was late because I had car trouble and didn't get started until late.

Foster: Did you see anyone enter or leave the premises?

Mr. Evans: I thought I saw their handyman, Randy Williams, driving his old pickup truck on the road ahead of me going toward Lizella.

Foster: Can you tell me the make and model of the truck?

Mr. Evans: I believe it is a 1968 Ford F100. I am certain because I had one of the same year, dark green. I traded it in last year for another one.

Foster: What color is Williams's truck?

Mr. Evans: It is a light blue, powder-puff blue, I think they call it. Not a man's color.

Foster: What tags did it have on it?

Mr. Evans: Georgia tags, Crawford County.

Foster: You're sure of this? Were you able to catch any of the tag numbers?

Mr. Evans: Yes, I'm positive, and no, I don't have any memory of the tag numbers.

Foster: Did his leaving at that time of day strike you as odd?

Mr. Evans: No, I sometimes saw him leaving in the afternoons.

Foster: I thought you said that your route brought you to the Forrester house before noon?

Mr. Evans: That's correct, but my return trip back to the Post Office is in the afternoon, so I pass the house every day.

Foster: So Williams was often at the house?

Mr. Evans: I wouldn't say 'often,' but he did do general yardwork for them.

Foster: Is there anything else you noticed?

Mr. Evans: No, when I got here, I heard Daniel and Patsy wailing. Terrible, there was blood on their clothes because they had walked through the blood. It was awful. I called to one of Forrester's neighbors, Mrs. Griswold, who was walking her dog and yelled for her to call the police.

Foster: Did you touch anything in the house?

Mr. Evans: Other than opening the front door, I don't think so, but I was so rattled that I may have.

Foster: Did you go into any other room?

Mr. Evans: Officer, I am so rattled by this I can't say for sure; I may have gone into the kitchen.

Foster: Did you touch anything?

Mr. Evans: Oh, I don't know; I may have. I am so upset that I can't remember anything.

Foster: Describe the scene when you entered the house.

Mr. Evans: As I said before, when I entered, the children were crying. I noticed that Marisa was on the couch at one end. John was at the other end. The room was unbelievably bloody, Marisa especially. I went outside with the two kids, as I said before, and yelled to Amanda Griswold to call the police. Then I waited for the police to arrive.

Foster: Do you own any firearms?

Mr. Evans: Yes, I have two rifles and two handguns.

Foster: Would you be willing to let me bring them to the station for examination?

Mr. Evans: Yes, but am I a suspect?

Foster: At this point, we are gathering information. What calibers are your firearms?

Mr. Evans: I have a Remington .222, and the other is a Winchester .308. The handguns are .22 and .32.

Foster then made a side note that he and Evans went to the postman's home. Evans went into the house and brought out the firearms.

Foster: After ballistics tests, we will return them to you.

Mr. Evans: Thank you, Detective Foster.

Foster: Thank you, Mr. Evans; I may have more questions for you later.

Mr. Evans: I hope you catch the bastards that did this.

"I'll read to you Detective Foster's notes after the

interview:

'Evans seems calmer than I would expect for someone coming upon a scene such as this. For some reason, I feel that he may be feigning his distress, but I could be wrong; people don't always act the way I predict they will. Other than some blood on his hands and clothes from picking up the children, there were no noticeable cuts that I could see. I have told Green that we should re-interview him soon.' "

"I thought that perhaps the re-interview report got misfiled; I have searched, but I can't find one," Sarah concluded.

"That is strange; Detective Green was always very thorough when I knew him. It is odd that he didn't follow up on Detective Foster's comments," Karen mused.

"I could have missed something, Karen, but I don't believe that I did. I have been through every binder in the case files."

"Well, perhaps Green didn't agree with Foster and decided not to act on it," Richard added.

"Possibly, but it isn't the Green I knew," Karen said.

"I am surprised that Foster didn't go into the Evan's house. Evans had blood on his clothes and shoes, he should have taken them for blood testing. Today we would have done DNA tests," Susan ventured.

"Also, when they were at Evan's house, Foster could have spoken to Mrs. Evans, but there is no record of that, then or later," Sarah added.

"What about the ballistics tests on the firearms?" Susan

asked.

"Foster's notes indicate that only the .22 caliber handgun was tested because the ME found that the bullets taken from Marisa and John were all .22 calibers, so there was no point in testing the others," Sarah responded.

"Did Foster say anything about checking Evans for any weapons on him that day when they were at the Forrester house?" Richard asked.

"Not I can tell from the notes," Sarah answered.

"Did Green have a gunpowder residue test done on Evans?" Karen asked.

"There is no indication in the records that one was ever done," Sarah responded.

"Maybe this is one of the holes in the original investigation that we are looking for," Karen said.

"Something tells me that we need to take another look at this Evans and his wife," Susan advised.

"Okay, let's check that out; let's see if we can talk to them," Karen directed.

"Was this 'handyman' ever found?" Richard asked.

"If he was, I can't find anything in the case files about interviewing Randy Williams," Sarah answered.

"This case was messy back then and now they want us to solve it after thirty plus years?" Richard asked.

"Okay, okay, we are beginning to find problems with the case. We have to explain or solve them, if we can. First, let's deal with Robert Evans while we try to locate Randy Williams," Karen ordered.

* * *

"Karen, we've located Robert Evans; he moved to the Tampa Bay area, Saint Petersburg, after retiring from the Post Office," Susan said.

"Has anyone talked to him?"

"I had a brief conversation with him by phone today. I asked if we could come out and talk with him. He agreed, but said that his wife is very ill."

"Is anyone willing to make the trip?" Karen inquired.

"I'll volunteer to drive out to talk to them, Karen," Susan said.

"Thank you, Susan. You have enough with your family. I'll go. I'll coordinate with the St. Pete Police. I'll plan to leave tomorrow afternoon after our morning meeting. See you then."

"I have some other news also, Karen."

"We have sort of located Randy Williams," Susan replied.

"What do you mean 'sort of?'

"We've located his ex-wife. Her name now is Anna Smithson; she remarried. She lives in Milledgeville and is willing to talk to us."

"How about him?"

"According to her, he was ill in 1995, but she doesn't know what was the cause. Apparently, it was not fatal because she talked to him a couple of years later."

"Does she know if he is still alive?"

"She hasn't had any contact with him since 2004."

"That's too bad, but she may be able to help to explain

a few things."

"Does she know where he may be living now, if he is still alive?"

"She has an address in Jacksonville where he was living for awhile. She doubts that he is still there; he tended to move every few years. They were married in 1976 and were divorced ten years later, but it may be worth talking to her," Susan responded.

"Well, I have a hunch that she is worth a visit. Would you drive out to Milledgeville and interview her?"

"I will call her back and set up a time."

"Great, Susan. When you get Randy's address from her, call Richard. I will have him make plans to interview Williams, if God willing, he is still alive and lucid."

Chapter Ten

"Mr. Evans, thank you for agreeing to see me on such short notice," Karen said after her introduction.

"I am always willing to help. It has been many years since that awful day in Middlefield, so my memory may be a bit foggy. What is it you want to know?"

Karen looked at Robert Evans and tried to picture him when he was in his prime. A wedding picture sat on a catchall table next to a comfortable looking chair. It was clear that Robert had been a catch for Arlene some thirty years ago. He was still a rather good-looking man today, but the youthful face had given way to years of living and showed lines that come with age. Slightly stooped, he looked like a man who had seen much during his life, not all of it good.

"I hate to remind you of the day back in 1979, but our records are not complete. Some of the investigator's notes have been muddled by age. Could you give me a brief bio of you and your wife?" Karen suggested.

"I can, where would you like me to start?"

"Not to be coy, Robert, but at the beginning," Karen answered.

"Okay. My wife, Arlene, and I lived on Parker Street in Lizella. By the time of the horrible murders, we had been married nine years, and had two children who were six and seven years old at the time. Arlene had been a stunning catch for me. She was taller than I, but that did not bother me in the least.

"We had met at a social event in Middlefield in our last year at Lizella High. Arlene had beautiful facial features with long dark brown hair and dark eyes which captured me from our first date. What she saw in me her friends could not figure out, but we were genuinely happy. No one could fault that. In any event, we didn't care what friends thought. But sometimes I still wonder what she saw in me. Her parents weren't sure about me, but in the end they came to appreciate me and, of course, eventually the grandchildren.

"After graduation, we both attended college and I earned a degree in Mathematics, and Arlene in English. I took my degree and applied for a teaching position at Lizella high school. To my great surprise, I was offered a position teaching. The reason I say 'great surprise' is that the principal had a policy against hiring former students, for some reason. But even more astounding was that Arlene also landed a position at Lizella teaching in her field. Old Watkins must have been losing it by the time we applied.

"Arlene and I married within a year after college, June 15th; we found a home to purchase; and began our careers. Our first child, Nancy, came along within the second year of marriage.

"But my stint in my chosen career path had lasted for only two years before I told Arlene that I had reached my limit working with uncaring students and I turned in my notice. We both understood that with one child already and another one on the way, life would substantially change. We knew that with the additional child, Arlene would have to give up her job also.

"I panicked and finally sat for the postal exam, which I passed. One month later I was hired by Uncle Sam and began my life as a mail carrier. Giving up teaching math was one of the hardest decisions I ever had to make, but my marriage and my children were the most important things in my life.

"Over time, Arlene and I had become friends with the Forresters. I had been their rural delivery mailman from the time John and Marisa had purchased their home in 1971. Over the next few years, we had become a little closer to them.

"We sometimes got together for barbecues at their home or ours on a Saturday afternoon. Our children were older by then and they were just having their family.

"At times, I would stop and talk to Marisa on my mail rounds. There was nothing sinister about that. I would sometimes share Marisa's problem of the day with Arlene who would then also talk with Marisa and give advice. Both women became really close and shared stories of their lives without embarrassment.

"One time, Marisa had intimated to me that John had periods of jealously that was sometimes directed toward many of Marisa's male friends, including me. I had been astounded at the suggestion. Compared to John Forrester, I was no physical match and no threat at all. I only stood five foot eight inches tall. John towered over me and had the physique that could break me in two. I had less than a robust build, which would be no match for John.

"That put an end to my talks with Marisa because of my fear of John. It also changed our family get-togethers. Eventually the barbecues stopped.

"Often, in the course of delivering mail to them, I could hear loud arguments coming through the walls as I brought their mail to the front of their house. Trying to be a gentleman and to avoid trouble, I politely put the mail on the porch and moved on with my route. The only person I mentioned this to was Arlene."

"When you discovered your grim finding that day, was Detective Foster the officer who interviewed you that day, if you recall?"

"I do, very well. Detective Foster was the first officer to that horrible scene."

"Yes, his notes say that you were able to identify the truck Randy Williams was driving away from the murder scene. The detectives, at the time, searched the DMV data base for the truck you described. They could find no match that tied the truck to Williams."

"I'm sure it was a blue pickup. I had one just like it. I traded it for a new truck."

"Yes, it was strange that it could not be located. You were sure that it had Georgia tags, right?"

"My memory is not what it was but, yes, I think I was very sure at the time."

"Was there anything else in your association with the Forresters?"

"Well, he and I were in the same gun club and sometimes went shooting together; just target, I hate to kill animals. He would ask me to go with him and most of the time I went, but I was never sure why he invited me, especially after our two families drifted apart.

"Frankly I was afraid of him. He invited me once to go hunting with him, but I never hunted. John was an avid hunter. Eventually, I resigned from the gun club."

"Was that the reason your families 'drifted apart?' "

"For me, yes."

"Did your wife and Marisa stay close friends?"

"Yes, they did; Mae and Arlene got together sometimes for lunch and conversation."

"Mae?"

"Yes, that was Marisa's name to her friends."

"I apologize for bringing this up, but my detective said that your wife is ill," Karen gently probed.

"Yes, Arlene is fighting something that the doctors have not been able to diagnose very well. She is very weak."

"I am sorry, Robert. Is she able to speak with me?"

"I would prefer not if that is all right. I think that whatever it is affecting her, is affecting her mind."

"I understand. It is okay."

"Did you know Randy Williams?"

"I can't really say that I knew him. More like I knew of him. I would see him often during the last several months before that terrible day, but we generally didn't speak. However, one time he stopped me when he was working at the Forresters' home to ask if I wanted to sell my truck. I told him no."

"Is that the only time you spoke to him?"

"As far as I can remember, yes."

"Were there any rumors about the Forresters and Randy?"

"I heard a vicious one about how he had tried to force himself on Marisa some time earlier that year. I believe it was a couple of months before the murders."

"There is nothing in the case files about that. Do you have an idea why?"

"I would have no idea about that."

"Did Marisa ever tell you the Williams' story?"

"No, she didn't. Maybe she was embarrassed."

"I am a bit surprised that she didn't tell you since you shared things."

"After the murders, I often wondered why she hadn't said anything to me, but…"

"Well, how did you hear of it?"

"It was common knowledge to the neighbors, so it got passed on to me. The rumor was that Mae had not done anything to lead him on. The rumor was that Marisa had told Williams not to do any more work for them. That was rumor also, so I really don't know what if it was true or not.

"I heard that John wanted him fired, but Mae let him keep doing the odd jobs. I don't know if John knew that.

Mae did tell me that one day on my route."

"If you were aware of this rumor involving Williams, why didn't you tell Detective Foster at the time?"

"It was a terrible rumor. I hate spreading rumors."

"If Arlene and Marisa were still close friends, wouldn't Marisa have told her about Williams?"

"She probably did, but Arlene kept it to herself. Wives don't tell their husbands everything, sometimes."

"That's true, but since you had heard the rumor about Williams and Marisa, I am surprised that you didn't bring it up with your wife."

"If I remember it correctly, I did try to talk about it; she told me to mind my own business about it. I'm still not sure why she said that, but it led me to believe that it must have happened."

"I hate to ask again, but I do need to speak with your wife. I need to clear up this point."

"Let me see if she is awake."

Evans walked to his wife's bedroom; Karen heard him gently awaken her.

"Detective Hunter, please come in."

Karen came into a pleasantly light room decorated with flowery patterned curtains adorning the three windows. The carpet, curtains, and wall colors were pleasingly matched giving the room a warm feeling. Mrs. Evans sat up in bed and reached her hand out as Karen moved to the side of the bed.

Karen could see that the person in the bed had been a

beautiful woman in her early days. Time and disease had stolen her youth and good attractiveness, leaving only a husk of the woman she once was. That she was well cared for went without saying. Karen thought that she must have been a strong character in her younger days.

"Arlene, this is Detective Hunter. She needs to ask you a question."

"Arlene, did Marisa ever mention to you an incident of Randy Williams trying to force himself on her?"

"Who are you again?"

"Detective Hunter from the Middlefield Police."

"What was the question?"

"Did Marisa ever mention to you an incident of Randy Williams trying to force himself on her?"

"Marisa? I can't remember. Who are you again?"

"Thank you, Arlene. You were a great help," Karen lied.

Leaving the sickroom, Robert said, "I'm sorry, Detective, you can see she doesn't have her faculties."

"I am sorry, Robert, I have a few more questions for you and then I will be done. Detective Green suspected Randy Williams to be person responsible for the murders, but over the years, he had not been able to develop any direct evidence to implicate him. After the murders, he disappeared. In your rounds, did you ever hear anything more about Williams?"

"I'm sorry, just the usual gossip, but nothing substantial. So no."

"I hate to take you back to that day again, Robert, but

you told Detective Foster that you may have gone into the kitchen and touched the countertop."

"I don't remember that for sure, but if you say I did, then I must have."

"There were two bloody fingerprints found on the countertop. Both were somewhat smeared, but there was enough clarity to give useable results.

"Detective Foster had you come to the station to give your fingerprints; one of the two prints on the countertop was matched to your right index finger."

"I was so distressed that day, I may have touched things that I shouldn't have. I picked up the children; they were covered with blood. Maybe that's how I got blood on my hands. It was the first time I had ever seen a murder scene."

"I'm not here to accuse you of anything, Robert; it is just that your print was there."

"I must have gone into the kitchen, but I was so rattled that I didn't remember it. If my print was there, I must have; I don't remember why."

"I understand."

"What about the other fingerprint? You said there were two. Was the other one ever matched to a suspect?"

"I can't talk about that print. Is there anything that may have come to you over the years that you didn't recall that day?" Karen said ignoring his question.

"No, if I had, I would have come to the station and told Detective Foster. I promised him that I would do that."

"Did that ever happen?"

"No, after the first few days, I was never in contact with the police again."

"Last question, can you put together a list of the people on your route at the time of the murders?"

"It will take me a little while, but I think I can. It's been a long time."

With that, Karen decided it was time to leave.

"Thank you very much, Robert, I think I've taken enough of your time."

"Robert, who are you talking to?" came a weak voice from another room.

"I'm talking to a nice lady from Georgia. She had a few questions for me. She is leaving now."

"When she leaves, please rub my back; it is so painful."

"I'll be right there, Arlene. I'm sorry, Detective, I must go to her."

"Thank you for your time, Robert. You have been very helpful; I may need to call you again sometime in the future, if that is alright."

"That is fine, anytime."

Chapter Eleven

The trip to Milledgeville was uneventful. Traffic was light and Susan managed the normal two-hour drive in faster time than she had expected to reach the Lakecrest Drive NE address.

"Anna has certainly moved up in the world," Susan thought as she drove up the well cared-for drive to the house. The home had been built in the boom of the late nineties in the southern style of the period.

As Susan exited her car, she recognized the care that the Smithson couple lavished on the flower beds and grounds. The house exterior was well-maintained and spoke of the character of the occupants.

Anna was waiting at the entrance and welcomed Susan into the foyer. As Susan looked around, she was struck by the décor representing the lifestyle of the couple. The furniture was expensive, but the home exuded an aura of lived-in comfort.

"Mrs. Smithson, thank you for agreeing to talk to me today. I appreciate your taking time out of your busy day to see me."

"That is quite all right, Detective. What can I do to help?"

"I hate to dig up the past in this way, but I need to find out more about your first husband, Randolph Williams," Susan began.

"Call me Anna, please; also, Randy could not stand the

name Randolph; no one called him that except his mother."

"All right, Anna. I need to know a little bit more about your life with him. What your lives were like before you married; you know, that kind of thing."

"Let me start here; I was born in Tennessee, a little town called Millington. My father was a Navy Lieutenant and we moved around from the time I was three years old, so what you might call roots are foreign to me. Don't get me wrong, Detective, my mother and father were very good to me and my sisters. They were strict about boys and dating, but they were always supportive. We had a good life.

"I met Randy when I went to Savannah on vacation with a group of high school girl friends after graduation. We met in a bar on River Street; he was in the Army at Fort Stewart. I had grown up around officers; so talking to an Army corporal was a new experience. His language and way of talking about things made a young girl's heart throb.

"He was from Jacksonville, Florida. He told me about his early life, which wasn't like anything I had experienced. He said his folks were poor; seemed like they just made ends meet. His father worked in a garage fixing cars. His mother took care of his brothers and sisters. My understanding from what Randy told me was he couldn't wait to get away from there. He never finished high school, but to his credit he did get his GED once he found out that he couldn't enlist without it.

"He was three years older than I was. We started dating and one thing led to another. He was a great lover and I thought I had found my man. You guessed it. I got pregnant; my folks were livid and insisted we get married.

"I thought it wouldn't be so bad; he did have a job and could take care of me and the baby. After we were married, he took me to meet his parents. I had insisted on it. It didn't seem important to him if they approved of me or not. I understood once we went there. His folks lived in a rundown trailer in a trailer park that had been in dismal shape twenty years before I set foot in it. Neither of his parents were very warm to me, which was just as well because at that time, I was starting to bulge out in front.

"Would you describe him as jealous?"

"He was; early on, that was one of the silly things that I thought proved he loved me. Later I realized it was just part of his macho character. He isolated me from my friends and I'm sorry to say, even my family."

"I'm sorry, Anna. Please continue."

"Seven months into my pregnancy, I miscarried. I never was pregnant after that, not that Randy didn't try. We moved to another base and then Randy decided that he didn't want any more of the Army.

"We moved from Washington to Jacksonville and lived there for a time. Finally, we moved to Middlefield where Randy was doing gardening work for families. He didn't have many skills, but the man could talk a plant out of the ground. People seemed to love him. Maybe too much. I suspected that he wasn't being faithful to me, but I couldn't prove it and he denied it. He was spending a lot of time at the Forresters' home."

"Was John Forrester home during these times?"

"I don't think so. He worked at gun place, I think. I really didn't know them. He was always enthusiastic about working for them and their neighbors, the Griswold family, however something changed with him in the Spring of that year. He got moodier that usual."

"Do you know what brought this situation on?"

"He said something happened at the Forresters' home that shouldn't have happened. When I asked him to explain he just shrugged his shoulders, but he said that he thought she was coming on to him. She rebuffed him; he accepted that and apologized to her.

"I believed him. Apparently, Mrs. Forrester had said something to her husband because he told me that his job there was in jeopardy."

"When did this happen?"

"I remember it clearly; it was in March of 1979. We had been married for five years. Things went on as normal for us after that for some time. We were having our own problems and his admission that things were not right with the Forresters just made everything worse."

"Did he stop working for the Forresters?"

"No, but he said that Mrs. Forrester had told him that her husband wanted her to fire him. She told Randy that she was not firing him. He only worked one day a week for each of his clients. Also, he continued to garden for families in that area, so I don't think whatever happened with Mrs. Forrester was that big a deal."

"Then you don't think he was having an affair with Mrs. Forrester."

"I really don't. Randy had a wandering eye like many men, but honestly, I don't think she was that type. As I said, I believed him. No, I didn't think so then or now. However, my trust in him was severely strained later in our marriage. I felt sure that he often cheated on me, but not with her."

"Were you aware that she was pregnant when she was murdered?"

"I had no idea about that. It was later when we were in Colorado that Randy told me that he thought she was at the time. He was quite upset when he told me. He said that she was just beginning to show. He swore that nothing ever happened between them."

"That's interesting, since the police never shared that information with the world."

"Well, it would make sense that he could have been aware of it. He did see her weekly before that terrible day. He had to get work instructions from her and pick up his pay. Are you now trying to tell me that Randy was the father?"

"We don't know that yet. We are looking at possibilities. It is becoming clearer that your ex-husband perhaps knew more than he told you. Can you tell me how Randy acted after the murders?"

"After the Forrester's murders, he was very moody. I could appreciate that; here was a woman he had labored for and talked with for a number of months. It was bound to be very upsetting.

"I know a detective interviewed him during that time. He was so upset that he couldn't sleep. They did grill him for several days. After they said he was free to go, we moved away."

"Did you think that he had anything to do with the murders?"

"He certainly never admitted anything like that to me. I would have called the police if he had. I wouldn't live with a killer. He told me that he was scared the police would try to pin the killings on him."

"Why did he believe that?"

"He got into some serious trouble in his early teens; I guess he figured that they would blame him, but they never arrested him."

"Anna would you excuse me for a moment?"

Susan went outside and sent an IM to Karen.

***

Karen, is there an interview record of Randy Williams in the case files?

***

Karen responded.

***

I'll have to check. I'll get back to you ASAP.

***

Susan returned and continued her interview.

"Can you tell me more about the day of the killings? Was Randy at the Forrester house that day?"

"Yes, that was the day he normally gardened for them. I dropped him off sometime mid-morning at the Griswold's. He had a small job to finish for them; then he said he would walk over to the Forrester's house to get his paycheck around noon or so.

"I was surprised because frequently he would work for most of the day at Griswold's and Forrester's. He normally split his time between the two households. Usually I would pick him up around five o'clock.

"When he told me that he was only going to the Forrester's to pick up his pay, I asked why. I asked him why he hadn't told me sooner; he finally told me that the incident 'that should not have happened' finally festered with her husband long enough. He told me that Mr. and Mrs. Forrester had a terrible fight over his continuing employment with them. Mr. Forrester had finally told him that they had no more work for him after that Wednesday. That was the day they were murdered."

"I am confused, Anna. Why would he have to return the following week to pick up his pay?"

"That was the agreement he had with all his customers; he worked a day; got paid the following week on that day. There was nothing unusual about that, but when he said that he needed to settle something with Mr. Forrester; I got worried; he had after all been fired. I warned him that he should not do that, but he wouldn't listen. I begged him; it was no use.

"It was then I thought that the thing, which had

happened was not quite what he admitted to me, but I never, ever thought someone would wind up dead that day."

"Just a curiosity question, Anna, why did you have to take him to work?"

"Usually, he would drive himself to the jobs in the old truck he bought earlier in the year…"

"So, at the time of the murders Randy owned a pickup truck?" Susan interrupted.

"Yes, but that day it was in the garage having something replaced. I can't remember what it was, so I drove him to work in our car."

"What was the color of your car?"

"If I remember correctly, it may have been white, but I couldn't swear to it."

"So, Randy did not drive the pickup truck at all the day of the murders?"

"I don't believe he did. After so many years, I can't remember when we picked it up after the repair, but it must have been later that day."

"Tell me a little more about the truck."

"Yes, we hadn't been able to afford one until some guy offered his old one to Randy for one-hundred bucks. It wasn't much to look at, but it ran. I never knew who he bought it from."

"Was it a powder-puff blue color?"

"Ha, ha, are you kidding me? Randy wouldn't have bought a truck that color. No, it was a dark green."

"Was it ever registered in Georgia?"

"No, Randy drove it to Florida a week after he bought it and registered it in Florida. He still had his Florida driver's license.

"Did Randy have any guns?"

"Yes, he and I both had .22 caliber Ruger. He always carried his with him. Mine was in my purse."

"Where is Randy's gun now?"

"I have no idea. He said he sold it after we came back from Colorado and moved to Florida."

"Do you still have yours?"

"Yes."

"Can I take it for ballistics checks?"

"Why? Am I a suspect?"

"Anna, this case has lingered for over thirty years. We are checking firearms belonging to anyone who was ever associated with the Forresters, even if your contact was only in an indirect way. I would like to be able to prove that your gun did not kill the Forresters."

Anna went to a desk drawer and brought out the .22 pistol.

Susan unloaded the pistol and put the bullets and gun into evidence bags.

"Where did you live when he worked odd jobs for the Forresters?"

"We lived in Middlefield in an old farmhouse on the outskirts of the city."

"You seem to have a very sharp memory of that day.

Why is that?"

"You would have too. When I drove into the driveway at the Forrester's house, Randy came running from the barn and we sped away. He was driving. When I asked him what was wrong, he said something terrible had happened to the Forresters.

"He had come to the door around just before noon to get his pay. He thought Mr. Forrester usually came home around that time for lunch. That was when he planned to talk to him.

"He told me that Mrs. Forrester invited him in, but he said he refused because Mr. Forrester was not home yet. Then she gave him his pay and he went to the barn to wait for John Forrester. While he was in the barn, something caused him to blackout. When he came to, he went back to the house, but he said that he heard voices yelling, so he ran back to the barn and stayed there until I got there."

"Did you believe him?"

"Detective Ramos, Randy's behavior really scared me. Randy did have strange blackouts that sometimes brought out a violent streak. He always claimed the blackouts prevented him from remembering what he had done. He later did tell me that he lied to the detective who questioned him. He said that he told him he never set foot in the Forrester house that day.

"Even though I could not believe that Randy had murdered the Forresters, the stress of living with his other problems finally forced me to make a decision. Two years after the murders, I divorced him."

"I'm not judging you, Anna. I have to ask these questions. Do you still think he had anything to do with the murders of the Forresters?"

"Honestly, I don't know. Maybe I just pushed the thought to the back of my mind so that I could function, I don't know. He certainly never admitted anything like that. I couldn't stand the idea of living with a possible murderer. That was probably unfair of me, but put yourself in my shoes."

"I understand. Are odd-jobs the only kind of work he did?"

"No, after Colorado, we moved to Jacksonville. He got a job as a school janitor and things went along well for a while, but the blackouts continued, so we parted."

"He didn't oppose the divorce?"

"No, I think it was a relief for us both. After that, I lost touch with him until I remarried. He sent me a letter of congratulations."

"Do you still have it?"

"I burned it the day I got it. Is there anything else you need to know?"

"Do you, by any chance, have anything that was a personal item for him?"

"What do you mean?"

"Something like letters he wrote or things he had handled when you were married to him."

"I understand; you're looking for fingerprints, or

something like that? Can't you just get them from him?"

"We will," Susan replied to Anna. "Once we are able to interview him," she thought to herself.

"I really have nothing. Well, wait a minute; he had a ponytail at one time. Before we moved from the area, he asked me to give him a haircut including lopping off the ponytail. He shaved his beard off.

"I know it sounds sophomoric and a bit silly now, but I liked his having the ponytail, so I saved a few strands. Don't ask me why; I still have them someplace. I will have to find where I put them. I did love him at one time, you understand. After I remarried, my husband was uncomfortable with my keeping things from my marriage to Randy, so I threw out everything I had except the hair."

"So you have no other things that he handled?"

"I don't know if I still have it, but Randy left a toiletry bag, which may be around here someplace. I will look for it and let you know."

"Well, thank you, Anna; if you can find the hair samples and the toiletry bag, we would appreciate it."

"I'll look for them; I'll get them to you as soon as I can."

"Thank you, Anna. I am sorry that I had to bring up old sorrows from that day."

"That's all right, Detective. It is a relief to tell someone about it. Randy said not to say anything about that day, so I've told no one."

"You were never interviewed at the time?"

"No, I was never asked."

Back in Middlefield, Susan and Karen discussed the interview.

"Karen, did you find the Williams interview notes in the file binders?"

"They are not in the files anywhere. I had Sarah and Richard take a look. They are missing."

"That's strange, Anna said that someone interviewed, well 'grilled' was her word, Randy for several hours. I can't imagine they're not there."

"I know. Green was a good detective. I have no explanation. We will keep checking. Does his ex-wife know where Williams is now?"

"The last Anna Smithson knew; he was still living somewhere in Jacksonville, Florida. That's where they were living when they divorced."

"We need to pay him a visit. I'll have Richard see if he can locate him and set up an interview."

* * *

Three days later, Anna Smithson sent Randy's hair samples and the toiletry case to Susan. The toiletry bag contained few items of interest to the investigation except for hair snagged on the hairbrush.

Items were sent to the GBI lab. The hair samples were not suitable for DNA analysis, but the lab chief said they could perform mitochondrial DNA tests. It would be a several week turnaround. Susan said that she understood; it was a long shot, but...

Chapter Twelve

"Morning, Karen, I've received the lab report of Williams' hair we sent to GBI. The strands had matching length, width, color, and scale characteristics of one of the collected hair samples. This matched a hair found on the chair next to the couch. That would make some sense; it may have come from his ponytail. We also have the mitochondrial test profile. Now if we can get Williams swab, we may be able to prove that his hair was at the crime scene. The hair was definitely from a Caucasian, but of course, physical hair forensics can't positively identify a person. But it helps us to pinpoint that sample from the chair."

"Yes, that may be, but unfortunately it doesn't prove it was dropped that day, nor does it really help our case. Williams was known to have been in the house at one time or another, but at least we can identify one of the hair's owners. It would be great if we could find the others."

"Well, the two hair strands found on Marisa and the one on John were quite different from Williams' hair, which was dark brown. Anna said Randy's hair color at the time was brown. She assumes that his hair has turned gray with age, but she hasn't seen him in years."

"That will be the major problem we have with these hair forensics. Thirty-plus years have changed individuals substantially. If we had to rely on physical characteristics alone, any samples we take today are probably of no value.

A defense attorney would tear our 'evidence' to shreds, but fortunately we don't."

"I agree, Karen, but we can't afford to test every hair found at the house."

"Of course, we can't, yet the most we will be able to do is speculate why the owners of the other samples had reason to be at the Forresters' home. However, our speculation is of no value; defense attorneys can speculate to sway a jury, but we can't, as you realize.

"Characteristics of any samples we take today have changed over the years from what they were that day. On that basis alone, there's nothing definitive that the DA can take to a Grand Jury, even if we believe that we have something, without a mitochondrial match to a suspect. As I said before though, that wouldn't prove the person was a killer."

"The hair samples of Marisa Forrester didn't match that phantom hair; I suppose?" Susan asked.

"Hairs were found from John, and the kids, throughout the house were taken and compared back then. They lived there. There were many others found in the house that belonged to Marisa. Her hair was long and black in color, so no.

"A blond strand was found on Marisa's shoulder. A third strand found on her chest was short in length; it had a reddish tint, but whose it was Green never determined. Another hair strand with the reddish tint was found on John's shirt."

"Karen, the problem with Green's investigation is that there's no record that the team took hair samples of the people they interviewed; there are no references in the reports of any physical forensic matching done at the time. I hate to say it, but Green was not as conscientious as I thought he was."

"Worse, Susan, he had no idea how many different people were in that house at one time or another; perhaps he thought that hair matching would be a waste of time. He might have thought hair forensics had more meaning depending on where a hair strand was found."

"I suppose you mean if a pubic hair was found on a victim's thigh or on, say, underwear."

"That's exactly what I mean. Simply finding a strand of hair in a room is of little value when many people have been there. That's why Green may have assumed that the blond strand found on Marisa's shoulder, and the strand found on her chest weren't considered key pieces of evidence. I think that was not unreasonable on Green's part. As we've said many times, back then they couldn't be used unquestionably to identify a person; they were of limited value in court," Karen declared.

"Well, then the only thing that we can say with certainty is that someone was close enough to Marisa that day to leave a bit of themselves on her."

"Also, Susan, looking back at the physical evidence reports, Marisa had had sex sometime earlier that day or the previous day; the semen was from a non-secretor.

Marisa's husband was a secretor, which as you know, constitutes a great majority of the population, so she was definitely having it on with someone else."

"Right, the post-mortem review also showed that she was a few months pregnant."

"When I last talked to Gordon about this case, Susan, he said that he still has frozen tissue samples from the fetus, Marisa, and John."

"How about the semen; did he preserve any of that?"

"He did. Perhaps it's time to spend some money and get whatever tests done we can. I can ask Gordon to process some samples."

"Are the samples still good enough to be tested?"

"Susan, we have to take a shot at it. The killer may still be alive, and if we can identify him; I want to find some solid evidence against him."

"Okay, I will get on it. I hope this is worth the effort and cost."

"We won't know until they are tested. The analysis processes are so much better than they were back in the seventies. I will send a message to Richard and Sarah for us to meet tomorrow morning; I'll let them know my plan about the DNA testing."

* * *

"Good morning. Susan and I went through the reasons that we should not place any great stock in the hair samples collected at the scene of the Forresters' murders. I would be happy to go over the rationale, if you wish."

"No, Karen, I also believe that it's a waste of time. Too many things have changed over the years. I am disappointed in the Green investigation, though," Richard replied.

"Without trying to defend him, Richard, I will say I thought he was a damn good detective."

"He certainly botched some important pieces of the evidence. I don't feel that he was such a great detective."

"You are entitled to your opinion, Richard, but let's move on. As you already heard, I have authorized some more DNA testing through Doctor Gordon on the Forresters' tissue and samples he has reserved. We should expect some results within a few weeks. We will also put a notice in the *Patriot* soliciting any information that anyone has about the Forresters' murders."

"Isn't a notice in the paper a waste of money, Karen?" Sarah asked, "Who is going to remember anything of value about that?"

"Possibly, Sarah, but something as significant as a murder, well, two murders, sticks in peoples' minds. I'm sure you all could tell me what and where you were and what you were doing when the World Trade Center buildings came crashing down."

"Yes, Karen, but that was such huge news. Murders happen every day; why would that stand out?"

"Richard, it might not, but I can give you an example of something that happened when I was only five years old. My mother and I were visiting a friend of hers in a small town. One afternoon, a neighbor three houses from where we were staying, was brutally murdered. She was knifed to death. As you may imagine, the news spread like wildfire and every neighbor was interviewed.

"The killer was never caught, but my imagination has kept that killing alive for over thirty-four years. I can remember what the house looked like, the time of day, the weather, and the knowledge, my mother told me, that the killer must have gone through the back yard of the house we stayed in."

"Karen, that is just the problem; your imagination has kept your impressions alive, not the facts," Richard asserted.

"But here's the rub in your argument, Richard, my mother swore that she saw the killer running through the back yard. She described him wearing a blue sport shirt and tan jeans covered with blood.

"She even noticed his hair color, black. She was a very good observer and even estimated his height. She tried to tell the police, but they were not able to do anything with it. She spoke very broken English with a heavy Italian accent; I guess that they didn't give what she told them much credence.

"I do know that they never caught the killer. The point is that she told me what she had seen; I have never forgotten it. There is someone, the Forresters' murderer, who our detectives missed back then; sad, but obviously true."

"Richard, the cost for the ad is small compared to what it might yield; I think it is worth a try," Susan said backing up Karen's contention.

"And the point is that other than some possible DNA results, we don't really have anything else to go on," Karen said.

"Right, and we would still have to match them with someone unknown at this point," Sarah interjected.

"Has anyone spotted anything else in what we have reviewed to date that Green and company may have missed?" Karen asked.

"I am a bit curious about Anna Smithson's conversation of the truck color that Randy had at the time. Didn't she say that the truck was a dark green color?" Richard recollected.

"Yes, Richard, when I interviewed her, she said without any hesitation that the truck was green; why is that important?" Susan responded.

"I believe it has importance because of the description that the postman gave," Richard answered.

"If I recall correctly," said Karen, "Didn't the postman tell Foster that the truck he saw leaving that morning was a blue one?"

"He did, but was he lying or was the stress of that morning playing tricks on him? We all know how unreliable eye-witnesses are," Susan declared.

"That is very true, and the more time passes the greater the error in the memory. We can't assume anything as to his lying to Foster or not," Karen responded.

"This process is beginning to wear me down. Things are standing out as flaws in what and how Green ran the investigation," Sarah said dejectedly.

"We must push on, Folks, we have no choice. I, for one, will not admit defeat. Two youngsters had their parents slaughtered while they were napping. They have borne this grief for many years; we need to provide some answers to them, whether or not we are tired or bored," Karen directed.

"I apologize, Karen, you are right," Sarah said.

"I suggest that we take a break from this work; meet in a week or so when the DNA results are done. We'll resume our work on this case, then. The break will give us all some relief, and I hope, freshen our spirits," Karen replied.

* * *

Three days later, Karen received a telephone call.

"Good morning, this is Major Hunter of the Middlefield PD. How can I help you?" Karen responded.

"Hello, I am calling in reply to the notice you put in the *Patriot*."

"Thank you for contacting us. What is it you want to tell me?"

"It has been many years since that awful day, but I still remember it like it was yesterday."

"What is it that you remember?"

"I was walking my dog, Blackie; oh, what a beautiful dog she was. Her coat was as shiny…"

"I don't mean to interrupt, but can you tell me more

about that awful day?" Karen pushed.

"If you'll give me a chance, I will tell you. Don't rush me or I'll hang up right now."

"My apologies, can you tell me your name?"

"I said to let me tell you my story or I will hang up."

"Okay, continue."

"As I said, I was walking my beautiful dog, Blackie. We were just crossing the Stillwater Bridge; you know back then, Mr. and Mrs. Forrester lived just a short distance from Stillwater Creek as did Franklin and I. We lived on the other side of the Creek.

"Well, Blackie started to go to the Creek, which she never did. When I looked at what interested her, I spotted something on the bank. It was a small accordion folder.

"I didn't know what it was, so I picked it up. Later, I took it home with me. While I was standing on the bridge, my postman, Mr. Evans, called to me to phone the police. Mr. Forrester was dead."

"It wasn't just Mister Forrester."

"I know that, but he was the nice one."

"What do you mean by that?"

"She wasn't as nice."

Karen decided to redirect the conversation to the folder.

"Did you open the folder?"

"I am not a nosy person, so I never looked in the package I found. I put it in our special place where we store valuable papers; it has sat there for over thirty years; actually I had forgotten about it. After your ad in the paper, I remembered it was there."

"Can you remember anything else about that day, Ms...."

"I told you not to interrupt me."

"I'm sorry."

"Yesterday I went to our special place and took it out. I'm afraid some mice have gotten into it over the years. Anyway, the folder is a bit chewed up, but you can have it."

"If you will give me your address, I'll have someone come out and pick it up," Karen offered.

"Don't have them come here at two o'clock, that's my nap time."

"I'll have a cruiser out there in twenty minutes. Is that all right?"

"Yes, but don't have them run their sirens; it scares my animals."

"Of course we won't, thank you for calling."

Chapter Thirteen

"Major, I must say that she is an interesting one," Officer Jones said.

"She sounded it on the phone; I thought that she was going to be 'nut case' number one calling, but perhaps this Miss Amanda Griswold has something we can use," Karen responded.

"She corrected me rather sternly, Major. It is Mrs. Franklin Griswold; she was never divorced; they simply separated. Her husband moved to Memphis over twenty years ago."

"I really did think she was a crank case," Karen replied.

"Here is the package, it looks pretty well chewed up. Hope it helps," Jones said.

When Jones left, Karen gingerly opened the small but tattered accordion folder. Inside were the remains of letters, but one had miraculously been not as chewed as completely by the ravenous pests. It was still partially complete. It was time to call the team together.

* * *

"Good afternoon, Folks. After our discussions about the usefulness of placing the newspaper advertisement, it seems that we may have gotten some results. A woman who was a neighbor in 1979 of the Forresters saw the ad and wanted to turn over some letters that she said she found on the day on the murders. She said that she stashed them away after that day without looking at them. I think the jury is still out on that one; I'll give her the benefit of the doubt, though.

"I want to share the letters with you, but I'll warn you that they are not in good shape. Her storage place for them wasn't mouse proof. In fact, only one has survived complete enough to gather any sensible information at all. Even that is not much; we will have to decide whether they have anything of value with respect to the Forresters' murders."

"Who is the mysterious person?" Sarah asked.

"She is Amanda Griswold, who lives in the same house she did back in 1979. She says that she found a package along Stillwater Creek on the day that the Forresters were murdered. She never told anyone about it or read the letters, so she says. As I said, I don't know if I believe her."

"Do you have the actual address?" Sarah asked.

"She lives at 1520 Old Albany Road, which is on this side of Stillwater Creek. Her house was only about a hundred plus yards from the Forresters. She said she discovered the package lying on the creek bank while she was on the bridge on that day."

"I'm with you, Karen, I don't believe that she didn't read the letters," Richard voiced.

"Although it is possible; she was thirty-five at the time and I doubt that she overcame any curiosity not to peek."

"Well, what does the letter say?" Susan asked.

"The date and address, if they were ever there, have been chewed away over the years. Other parts of the letter were also destroyed by mice chewing, but you will get the sense of it:

> *You are a piece of*
> *I am telling you,   had better stay away*
> *from my   I will ill you if   ry to*
> *see   ag in, your death is near. You are*
> *ruining my life. This is the last warning. You are*
> *a bastard and a homewrecker. I am going to*
> *your   You will not live to see   that*
> *bas   hild grow up.*
>
> *You know I mean every word. I am your*
> *worst nightmare, slut.*
>
> *A   a*

"This is a vicious letter; it had to have been written by a woman to Marisa," Susan said.

"I agree; it fits. The question is who this 'A' blank 'a' is," Karen added.

"Why do you assume it is written by a woman, Susan?" Richard pushed.

"If you can't see the imprint of a woman's mind at work, I feel sorry for you," Susan replied with some anger.

"Richard, I think it is a woman's way of attacking a foe, just saying. From what we've learned from Green's original investigation and ours, we have not run across anybody with a name starting with 'a' and ending with 'a'

143

who could have been involved with the Forrester's killings," Karen added.

"Are we forgetting Amanda Griswold, herself, Karen? She was involved in this whole matter in a way that we don't understand yet," Richard interjected.

"There is an Amanda Pierce who lived at 1514 Old Albany Road back then," Sarah added, "I'm just finishing the touch-up of Detective Green's old map of the street."

"Well, she's a possibility; maybe we should take a closer look at her," Richard added.

"That's true that she lived there then, but Sarah says she is in her late eighties now; my gut says that she was never entangled in the killings," Karen countered.

"Then who is this mysterious 'A' blank 'a'?" Richard asked.

"I'm not sure we will ever know," Karen answered.

"I can't believe that this Griswold woman didn't turn this over to the police back then," Susan said.

"Either she is telling the truth about not reading them, or she just didn't want to get drawn in, but I wonder if she does know who wrote the letters," Karen responded.

"Or, she was directly implicated somehow with the murders; perhaps she is the author," Richard ventured.

"I know; that will be difficult to prove, Richard."

"What about the other letters; you said there were more?" Sarah asked.

"The packet has two others; they have similar threats, but are also not in very good condition; in fact, they are much worse. They really are not readable at all."

"Is handwriting analysis of any value here?" Sarah asked.

"In my experience, probably not. Handwriting for individuals may change significantly over the years," Karen answered.

"That's true, but certain letters may still be the same," Richard pushed.

"Do you really believe that Amanda Griswold would turn them over to us if she had written them?" Susan asked.

"Probably, not likely," Karen said.

"Is she willing to talk to us?" Richard asked.

"We've got to talk to her," Susan said.

"Those are my thoughts exactly," Karen replied.

"How soon?" Richard asked.

"Very soon, but I think this should be a one-on-one interview at her place. When I talked with her on the phone yesterday, she was very waspish; we'll need our best interviewing skills to get her to speak truthfully," Karen answered.

"Who do you think should interview her?"

"I'm not saying that I am the best for this, but I think I will have a crack at it. If that doesn't work, we will haul her into the station," Karen replied.

"That could backfire if she is as crusty as you say," Richard added.

* * *

Karen arrived for her interview with Amanda Griswold;

145

studying the room where she was invited to sit. The living room, which faced south, was darkened by heavy drapes drawn on the three windows that looked toward Old Albany Road. Without modern air conditioning, it was a way to keep the home cooler by blocking out the summer sun in the afternoon.

The furnishings represented years of use and had not been updated. A doorway led to the kitchen, which in turn led into a dining room through a swinging door, which reminded Karen of those used in old western movies. The woodwork had been darkly stained years ago and hadn't seen a facelift in many years.

The whole house had a musty smell, which Karen recognized that many old houses seemed to have even though the odor was not due to uncleanliness.

Karen estimated that Amanda Griswold was in her late sixties. Short in height, and burdened with weight that accumulates over the years, she had a face that was surprisingly young looking. Overall, she seemed to be in good health.

"Ms. Griswold, thank you for agreeing to talk with me today. I have brought the letters that we picked up the other day. I would like to verify that these are the letters you spoke to me about on the phone."

"Please call me Amanda or Mrs. Griswold. I don't go for that new-fangled way of speaking to women."

"Okay, Amanda it is. Is your husband available to talk to me also?"

"No, he lives in Memphis; has for a long time. He lives with some sugar mama he met years ago."

"Are you divorced?"

"No, Franklin does not believe in it; he just wanted his freedom and left one day. I couldn't stop him; he still takes care of me financially, so I don't bad mouth him."

"Can you tell me anything more about the letters in the folder?"

"When Franklin got home, I was still outside talking to the detective. He found the folder and opened it up."

"So, you don't really know how many letters were in the folder?"

"He told me there were four letters."

"Did he say if there were any love letters?"

"He told me about the letters; there were four of them. As I told you on the telephone, I didn't read them."

"I want to believe that, but human nature is generally different. Our curiosity often gets the better of our principles. It certainly is not a matter to be ashamed of."

"I didn't want to snoop on someone. Franklin read the four letters and told me about them."

"Four? There were only three in the package you gave us."

"No, I clearly remember he told me there were four. I would appreciate it if you wouldn't argue with me."

"I'm not trying to argue with you, Amanda, but that means one is missing. Do you have any idea where it could be?"

"No, I don't. Perhaps it got misplaced over the years. I don't know. I do remember that it was different from the other nasty ones."

"What do you mean by nasty?"

"Franklin said three were full of hateful accusations and cussing."

"I hate to return to this, but I am confused, Amanda, didn't you just say that there were four letters?"

"That's what Franklin told me. He said that one was very different. It was in a foreign language."

"You know that the package you gave us only contained three. One badly chewed up and the other two not readable at all. Where is the fourth one?"

"I don't know; Franklin put the folder into our hiding place; I never looked in it until recently."

"Amanda, I am having a hard time believing you. I am certain that both you and your husband read the letters. It's only natural for people. I need to know who the letters were written to."

"I'm afraid I don't remember. I didn't read them."

"You are hiding something from me. What is it? Did Franklin tell you who they were addressed to?"

"No, Franklin said that there were no names, only horrible swearing. Franklin said…"

"I don't mean to insult you, Amanda, but I know that both you and Franklin read the letters. Stop lying to me."

"If I did, will you arrest me?"

"No, Amanda, but you must tell me everything you

know about the letters, or I will be forced to consider that both of you were involved in the murders of your neighbors."

"Please don't arrest me. I didn't do anything to the Forresters."

"You need to tell me everything about the letters and what happened that day. How did you know to call the police? Your name was given in the records as the caller."

"When I was on the bridge walking Blackie, she was such a sweet dog, our mailman yelled to me to call them. Back then, our side of the street didn't have as many trees as there are now. I could see the Forrester's home from the bridge at that time.

"He yelled that something horrible had happened at the Forresters' place. So I went home and called. My home is only a short distance from the bridge, as you know."

"Had you found the letters before going home to call?"

"Yes, I had the package in my hand when Evans called to me. While I was calling the police, I put the package next to the phone and then went back to the bridge."

"What happened next?"

"That day I found the package, in the excitement, I forgot about it and I didn't tell Franklin about it until he got home from work. A detective had stopped by the house late that afternoon, and I didn't tell him about the package."

"Yes, our records show that Detective Foster was the person who spoke with you. He asked you questions about the Forresters."

"Yes, I remember it well. I told him that I didn't know anything about their private lives."

"Was that the truth, Amanda?"

"Partially, he asked about any rumors I may have heard, but I told him I knew nothing. That was only partly true. There were some things I knew and things that I think happened.

"I told him that they were fine people and neighbors. Franklin would go over to their house sometimes to fix things that Mrs. Forrester said were broken."

"What kind of things?"

"Franklin was an electrician by trade, he was very handy about things. A few times she would call when we had bad weather; he would go over and help them get the electricity back on after one of those terrific thunderstorms. Usually a fuse or something needed replacing. Apparently Mr. Forrester wasn't a handyman.

"Franklin loved to help people. I did feel funny about Mrs. Forrester always needing help from Franklin, but I kept my thoughts to myself. I can tell you it did make me mad sometimes."

"Angry enough to do something about it?"

"Of course not; I couldn't hurt anyone."

"Did you and Franklin own any guns?"

"Yes, he had some for hunting."

"How about pistols, did you two own any?"

"I think he did, but don't ask me where they are. I don't have any idea."

"Well, Amanda, tell me about what was in the letters. Since you read them, I would like to know."

"There were no names in the letters that I recognized, so I can't help you there. Whoever wrote them threatened to kill her, but you couldn't tell because the language was so vague except for the threats themselves.

"Franklin said that from the letters, it sounded to him like someone must have been seriously involved with Mrs. Forrester, if you know what I mean. Because I had fibbed to your detective, I was afraid that I might be arrested.

"After we had read the letters, we were terrified that whoever killed the Forresters would come after us. I didn't know if the killer saw me pick up the package. That's all I can say about them. Franklin didn't want to get involved and so we put them in our safe place."

"Were there only hateful letters. Amanda?"

"What do you mean?"

"I am asking again, were there any love letters?"

"Franklin took charge of the packet so I don't rightly know."

"I don't believe you Amanda. You know there were other letters and you did read them. Were the letters written by your husband?"

"I have no idea. I didn't see or read them. Franklin was nervous about the package of letters; I honestly don't know if they existed."

"Do you believe that there was anything going on between Franklin and Mrs. Forrester?"

"I thought that there might be at the time, but I didn't want to accuse Franklin. I thought it curious with all those fuses blowing out, but. I didn't dare question him about it. My suspicions led to our separating eventually."

"Did your husband kill the Forresters?"

"No, no, no. I know he didn't."

"How do you know?"

"He swore he didn't; I believed him."

"Where was he on the day of the murder?"

"He was at work. He came home for lunch around eleven thirty and usually went back after one."

"Was he with you the entire lunch time?"

"Yes, well no, I drove to the grocery store and he had left by the time I got back."

"So you can't say for certain that Franklin did not go over the Forresters during this time, nor what time he left."

"No, I guess I can't."

"I didn't ask you earlier, but what time were you walking your dog that day?"

"I usually walked her just before my lunch, that is, about twelve. We would walk down to the creek and go past the Forresters' home and back, about a half hour walk."

"You need to answer my question. What time did you start your walk that day?"

"Because I went to the store, I didn't start my walk until about quarter to one."

"Did you see anything unusual that day before the mailman yelled to you?"

"I told your detective that I didn't, but I remember seeing a vehicle off in the distance going towards Lizella. It was an old truck, like the one the handyman had."

"What handyman was that?"

"I think it was Williams. Franklin got angry with him when he did work for us. Franklin said he did sloppy work, but that wasn't the real reason. He was very jealous and he saw the way Williams looked at me sometimes; he didn't fire him, but he was close to it."

"What do you mean about the way he looked at you?"

"You know, you're a woman, how a man looks when he's undressing you with his eyes. Franklin got very angry and told him to knock it off."

"So, you believe that you saw Williams truck leaving the Forrester home and you didn't tell the detective that day?"

"No, it has haunted me since that time."

"It should have, Amanda, because it perhaps allowed a murderer to get away."

"I know. I am very sorry."

"I'm curious about something that the detective who interviewed the mailman said on the day of the murders. He told the detective that he saw a powder-blue truck leaving the Forresters' house as he approached it. Why do you suppose he made that mistake?"

"I don't know. I remember the truck as green."

"It is obvious that one of you is mistaken. Why do you suppose that is?"

"I didn't tell about the truck, because I was afraid that the killer might come back for me."

"It is time for you to tell me the complete truth, Amanda."

"I did see the green truck leave, Williams's truck, I think. I swear it was green, but before Mrs. Williams came to pick up her husband, I saw a white car leave the Forresters."

"Did you tell the detective about that?"

"No, I told you I was scared."

"Did you ever tell anyone in authority about what you saw?"

"No, our mailman, Mr. Evans, asked me what I saw several days later and I told him about the truck. He was the only one. I never mentioned the white car to anyone except Franklin."

"Why was that?"

"I got flustered with all the commotion; Franklin said the killer may have seen me; perhaps he would come back and kill me. I was afraid after that."

"Was it a man or woman driving the car?"

"Even today I am not sure; I wouldn't dare say; I just don't know."

"You may have held the key to solving their murders and yet you kept silent. That is pretty disgusting, Amanda."

"I know; I am so sorry."

"Is there anything else that you can tell me about the Forresters?"

"Not really, except that I heard that they sometimes were not as devoted to each other, if you catch my drift."

"You're saying that they were unfaithful to each other?"

"Only some rumors I heard, not proof, just saying."

"What were the rumors?"

"Only that he was messing with someone and she found out."

"And, of course, you don't know who."

"No, sorry, I don't."

"Do you have your husband's address in Tennessee?"

"Let me get it for you. I have it in my desk."

"Alright, thank you, Amanda, if you can think of anything else, please give me a call. Here is my card. Thank you for your time.

"In the future, if you are aware of something and you are asked about it, tell the truth. What you did back then was to obstruct the course of justice. If you had been truthful, it may have allowed us to apprehend the killer. Your silence cost the investigation much useless time.

Chapter Fourteen

"How did your interview with old lady Griswold go?" Richard asked.

"At first, not too productive, but she eventually came clean about her story of the letters. More importantly, she said that she lied to Green's crew back then."

"What do you mean?"

"She told me that she didn't tell them about a white car she saw leaving Forresters' house just before Randy Williams's wife came to pick him up. William's story was that when he went to the house to get his pay, he heard loud arguing and ran to the barn until his wife picked him up."

"I think that we should arrest her," Richard said.

"For lying over thirty years ago? Get real, Richard," Karen answered.

"Does she know where her husband is now?" Susan asked.

"He lives in Tennessee. I have his address. We need to call him. Is his interview report in the case files?"

"I checked," Susan said. "After the Williams' problem, I got worried. It is there; I will say it is pretty bland. I can see why he was never seen as a suspect, but we need to ask him why he may have lied in the interview."

"After this meeting, we will set up a visit with him. It's expensive, but we have to interview him face-to-face," Karen directed.

'What did happen that day?" Richard asked.

"When Detective Foster spoke with Amanda Griswold the day of the Forresters' murders, she lied. Well, she lied, and so did he, by omission, by not revealing that she had found a packet of letters, which perhaps had a connection to the murders. She and her husband, Frank, read the letters and decided to keep quiet. She said that at the time they didn't want to become involved with the investigation, and they were scared the killer may have seen Amanda, but that reason still doesn't ring true to me."

"What is it that bothers you, Karen?" Susan asked.

"Honestly, I can't explain it, but I am beginning to appreciate the problems that Detective Green encountered thirty plus years ago."

"Do you believe that Amanda Griswold has more to say?"

"Perhaps, but it will take someone she trusts to get it out of her. Also, I want a thorough check done on Amanda Griswold's financial accounts over the past years," Karen commanded.

"Speaking of looking at old accounts, have any of the DNA tests results come back yet?" Richard asked.

"No, we are in a long que line because of this being a cold case," Sarah replied.

"Well, they could be very interesting. You remember that Doctor Gordon preserved blood samples from both the Forresters and from the fetus Marisa was carrying. What if there is a bombshell result that Marisa's baby was not John Forrester's?" Susan speculated.

"What?" Karen asked incredulously.

"It is a possibility, as you know back then we didn't have the techniques we have today. Green had to work with blood typing, which was advanced for the time, but wasn't as definitive as our tests today. Obviously something very serious drove these killings."

"Yes, Green's notes indicated that he had suspicions about the paternity of Marisa's child. If I recall correctly, Susan, John had B type and Marisa had type A blood. Even though it is not conclusive evidence, the baby's blood type was B, and that meant the baby's father had B blood type," Karen added.

"I forget, what were Daniel and Patsy's blood types?" Richard asked.

"Daniel is type A and Patsy is type O, matching what we might expect for two children of blood type A parents, but of course, John was B," Susan replied.

"Remember, the problem with all of that is that if one parent has B type and the other A, the child can be O, A, B, or AB, so you could have two kids with one having A and the other O," Karen warned.

"Can we find out what blood type Williams had?" Sarah asked.

"Yes, in reviewing Green's notes. Williams was active Army for two years, Vietnam for one year, and Green got his blood type, B, from his records," Susan answered.

"That could mean Williams could have been the father of Marisa's baby. That fact could have provided a reason for murdering her. Was John just collateral damage?" Richard speculated.

"I am afraid that is something we will never know, unless we can find Williams and get a bio sample to test."

"We need to call Anna Smithson to ask if she knew there was an affair between Randy and Marisa," Karen directed.

"No need. When I interviewed her, she said that she did not believe Randy and Marisa had an affair, except for the strange incident, which led to the row between him and John Forrester," Susan offered.

"Okay, thank you, Susan, I forgot that. Did the lab results come back for Williams's hair analysis?"

"They have, Karen, his hair is physically similar to the hair found at the murder scene, but the lab cannot conclusively say they match until the mitochondrial testing is completed," Sarah answered.

"Well, that is normal, but their ability to say that the hair is very similar is encouraging. We may be able to narrow the murders to him, although I don't have any idea how we will be able to prove it, yet."

"Well, let me give her a call anyway. It won't prove anything even if she did think they had an affair. He was very controlling; I doubt that she wouldn't have reported it if she felt he had killed them. Anna was quite emphatic about that," Susan said.

"Well, let's find out anything more you can from her. She can't be afraid after all these years," Karen answered.

"If she is silly enough to admit that she knew he killed

them, she was an accessory and we should arrest her," Richard said.

"Even if she does admit it, Richard, we are not going to arrest her. Tom Hansen could not build a case. It would only be her word that he had told her. Where's the proof?" Karen pushed back.

"You're right, Karen, I was just hoping for a break in this mess," Richard answered.

* * *

"I spoke with Anna Smithson. She said that she still does not think Randy and Marisa had an affair, but she said that, frankly, she couldn't know for certain one way or the other.

"She said again that he never admitted he had anything to do with the murders, but he did want to move out of town because he thought the police would pin it on him, sooner or later," Susan reported.

"Well, that seems to close out that angle, or does it?" Karen pronounced without conviction.

"This case is getting under my skin. I'm out of ideas to follow at this point," Susan uttered.

"I certainly hear you, Susan, but I sure hate to go to the Chief and cry uncle."

"What else can we do? Green conducted a reasonably thorough investigation even though we have discovered some problems. If he couldn't find out who the killer was when memories were fresh, how can anyone expect us to deliver an answer after thirty-four years?" Susan lamented.

"Well, before I see Tate, I will give our ad in the *Patriot* another few days to work. Amanda Griswold gave us some interesting information, but somebody out there knows more about the killings. I hope their conscience will force them to tell us. Let's give it a few more days before I have to call this investigation quits."

"Okay, Karen, I do regret that we couldn't provide an answer to those Forrester kids."

"That is life sometimes, but…"

Karen's phone rang with Richard nearly out of breath on the line.

"Karen, Amanda Griswold has been murdered. She has a friend, who delivers meals to her, who came to her home and found her."

"What, Richard, is going on in this town?" Karen asked with disbelief in her voice.

"I've already called Doctor Gordon. I took the 911 call and went out there. I can tell you it's a mess."

"Are the criminalists there?"

"Yes, they're doing what they do."

"Susan and I are on our way."

* * *

Reaching the Griswold home, Karen and Susan traversed the police crime scene tape strung around the driveway and entered the house.

Richard greeted them with, "As you can see, Karen, she was found in a chair in the living room."

"Yes, I can see."

"A nasty way to go," Richard exclaimed.

161

"Richard, when you called me, you said Amanda had been murdered. At first glance, this scene appears more like a suicide to me."

Amanda Griswold lay slumped back with her head skewed to her left side. Her eyes were still open and her mouth agape. Blood had run down from the bullet hole in her forehead, which was partially hidden by her hair and coursed its way over her nose and by her lips where it had dripped from her chin onto her day dress. Her right hand rested on her lap lightly gripping a Colt pistol.

"I find it interesting that she doesn't have a death grasp of the gun, but is loosely held," Richard continued.

"It looks as though she didn't have the cadaveric spasm we sometimes see in suicides," Karen answered.

"In this case, the .22 caliber recoil may not have been enough to cause it to be dropped," Richard offered.

"At this moment, Richard, I am just speculating."

Just then, James Gordon walked over to Karen and Richard.

"I overheard you and Richard just now. I'm not prepared to say it's murder or suicide until I complete a post-mortem."

"I understand, James. We will have the firearm checked for prints by the GBI Lab."

"In the meantime, I believe it would be prudent to consider this a homicide and handle it as such until I can tell you differently," the ME replied.

"Okay, James, that makes good sense. We will await

your decision. I will have someone at the post-mortem. What time?" Karen asked.

"As soon as the scene is wrapped up by the criminalists, I will have her moved to the morgue. I'll schedule a post-mortem for tomorrow morning, Karen."

"Thank you, James, let us know the time."

"I'll have my assistant call."

"Richard, have you spoken to the friend who found her yet?" Karen questioned.

"Just briefly, Karen; I asked her, Mary Ellen Conner, to come to the station to give her statement."

"That's good. Is there anyone else we need to interview?"

"Karen, we should interview all the neighbors on her street. There are five on this side of Old Albany Road and eight on the other side of the road," Richard responded.

"I agree, and it should be done today. You, Susan, and I will start as soon as we finish here," Karen directed.

"It's sort of ironic that the old Forrester place is just across Stillwater Creek to the right of this place," Susan commented.

"Yes, didn't she tell you that back when the murders took place she had a clear view of the Forrester's house from her home?" Susan queried.

"Well, it's all grown up in between them now," Karen replied.

"I suggest that we get moving; I'd like to finish our interviews while we still have daylight," Karen directed.

"Before you get started, Karen, Sarah updated Green's original map of the area.

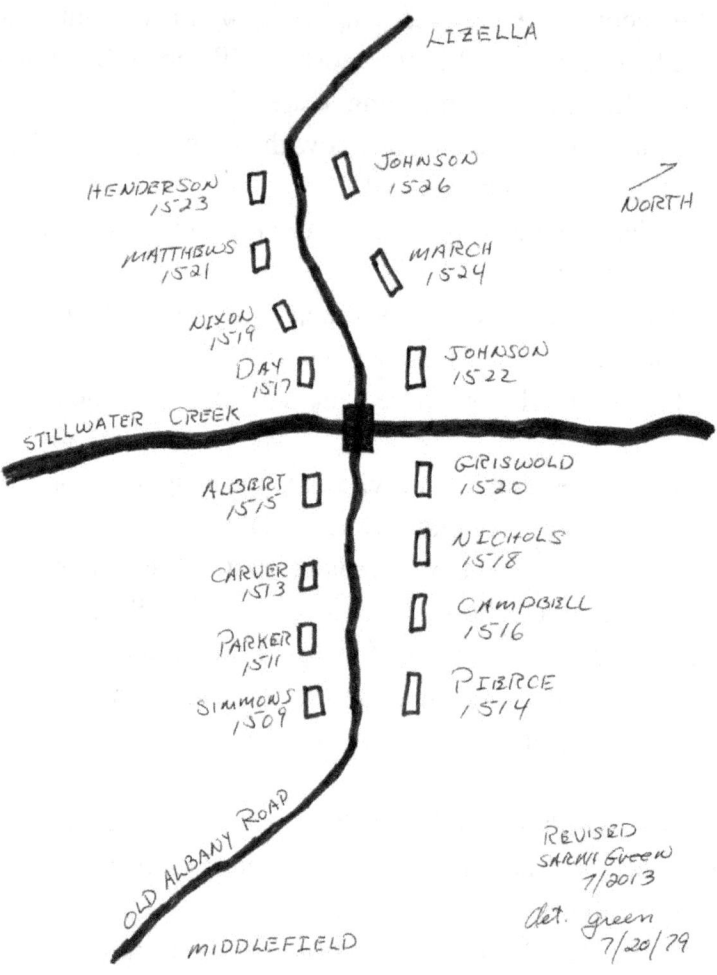

"She added the eight houses closest to the Griswold residence located on the opposite side of Old Albany Road, which were not there when Green drew the map in 1979. She gave them to me yesterday; I took the initiative to bring them before we left the station."

"Thank you, Susan. Let me take a look at it."

"You'll also notice that she also added the house numbers for all the homes, since they were not on his old map. Also, she updated the home owners' names; since some have changed over the years. I thought it might help; I also made copies for each of you," Susan explained.

"Thank you, Susan. I see two Johnsons are listed. I assume that they are related," Karen noted.

"I asked Sarah the same question; yes, Raymond, Jr. lives at house number 1526."

"We really need to find a way to promote Sarah. She is outstanding support for us," Karen declared.

Even with the help of the new map, the neighborhood interviews took the rest of the day and went into the early evening.

The MCU met for a few moments at the station to plan a review for the interviews to be done the next day.

Chapter Fifteen

"Good morning, Folks, I hope you all rested well last night. We agreed yesterday that we would review the interview results today. Let's get started. Susan, will you scribe for us?"

"Okay, Karen, who's first?"

"I'll start," Richard said, "I had four of the eight houses on the other side of the street from Griswold's on the Lizella side of Stillwater Creek."

"Okay, Richard, give us the house number first, then occupants' names."

"I will start with the house farthest from the Griswold home," Richard said.

1) 1523 Old Albany Road
   a) Henderson, Ruth
      i) Husband, James, deceased
      ii) Was at home but didn't notice anything out of the ordinary all morning
      iii) Drove to Middlefield at one in the afternoon
      iv) Saw Mary Ellen's car in the Griswold driveway on her way out

2) 1521 Old Albany Road
   a) Matthews, James and Rita
      i) James at work from 8 to 5 pm
      ii) Rita at home but didn't notice anything out of the ordinary all morning

      iii) Noticed a black Chevrolet in the Griswold's driveway at about twelve thirty in the afternoon

      iv) Saw Mary Ellen's car in the Griswold driveway around one o'clock

3) 1519 Old Albany Road
   a) Nixon, Arthur and Jane, both retired
      i)   Arthur said he saw a strange car driving up and down the street around ten
      ii) Noticed that a black Chevrolet pulled in Amanda's driveway around eleven
      iii) Thought he saw a tall, light skinned man go to her door
      iv) Thought the Chevy was a 2005 or 2006 Malibu, not certain
      v) Thought about calling the police, but didn't
      vi) Jane was home but had laid down because of a headache and didn't see anything
      vii) Saw Mary Ellen's car drive into the Griswold driveway about one o'clock

4) 1517 Old Albany Road (directly across the street from the Johnson home, or I should say, the old Forrester home)
   a) Day, Michael and Noreen
      i)   Michael was at work during the day
      ii) She is a seamstress and works at home in a room on the back side of the house
      iii) Noreen did not notice anything out of the ordinary that day, except when police arrived at Griswold's home

"Okay Richard, my turn. I had the next four houses on the opposite side of the street from the Griswold's house. The houses were part of a planned development that stopped when the economy went south. I'll continue with the houses on the Middlefield side of Old Albany Road. All of the houses I visited had residents who lived there less than five years, so I felt that questions about Amanda Griswold were probably not very reliable."

"Yes, I asked questions about the Griswolds, but no one admitted that they knew anything about Amanda's or Franklin's activities. They didn't socialize with them," Richard added.

"That was my experience also. Well, we were most interested in what they may have seen yesterday," Karen explained.

5) 1515 Old Albany Road
   a) Albert, David and Marie
      i) House is directly across the street from Griswold's home
      ii) David works nights at the Shell Station in Lizella
      iii) David saw a black Chevy in Griswold's driveway around noon
      iv) Saw a man leaving dressed in jeans and shirt
      v) Had not seen the man there before
      vi) Man was older, in his sixties, slightly balding

6) 1513 Old Albany Road
   a) Carver, Gerald and Mary
      i) Gerald was home with a broken ankle
      ii) He saw the black Chevy in Griswold's driveway around ten thirty
      iii) Saw a man sitting in the car
      iv) After a few minutes, the man went to the Griswold front door

7) 1511 Old Albany Road
   a) Parker, George and Lucille
      i) No one at home
      ii) Checked that both work and were at their Middlefield College jobs yesterday

8) 1509 Old Albany Road
   a) Simmons, Lucille
      i) House is the farthest from Griswold's home
      ii) Did not see anything unusual all morning
      iii) Only realized something was amiss when the police came to Griswold's house
      iv) She often has a mid-day coffee with Griswold. Sometimes at her house and others at Griswold's house

"That's about all I learned from my four; Susan, what did you find out?" Karen asked.

"On the Lizella side of Stillwater Creek are three houses, as you know. On the Middlefield side there are also three houses from Griswolds' home. I will start with the farthest house from the Lizella side of the Creek.

169

1) 1526 Old Albany Road
   a) Johnson, Raymond Jr. and Grace
      i) Grace was just getting home from her job and so saw nothing that day
      ii) Leaves for work by 8:30 a.m.
      iii) Husband, Raymond is on a business trip to Tennessee
      iv) Neither of the Johnsons knows Amanda Griswold except as a neighbor
      v) Raymond is the son of Mary Johnson who lives in what was the Forrester home

2) 1524 Old Albany Road
   a) March, Daniel and Nancy
      i) Daniel saw a black Chevrolet parked in Griswold's driveway around nine-thirty
      ii) Daniel is home on a disability and was going to the CVS in Middlefield when he saw the car
      iii) Nancy is a nurse at a Lizella nursing home and left for work around 5:30 a.m.

3) 1522 Old Albany Road
   a) Johnson, Mary
      i) Husband Raymond Sr. deceased
      ii) Son, Raymond Jr., lives two houses away
      iii) Reported seeing a white car in Griswold's drive around nine a.m.
      iv) First witness who saw a white car; others saw a black car (Chevrolet)
      v) She was out for some errands
      vi) She insists the car she saw was white

4) 1520 Old Albany Road
   a) Amanda Griswold's house

5) 1518 Old Albany Road
   a) Nichols, James and Martha
      i) Saw/heard nothing unusual at Griswold's home
      ii) Both work in Middlefield so their morning routine does not take them past Amanda's house
      iii) Have lived next to Griswolds for thirty years
      iv) The couple does not socialize with Amanda Griswold
      v) Had a falling-out with Amanda's husband, Frank, some years ago
      vi) Apparently Frank had a roving eye and made some suggestion to Martha

6) 1516 Old Albany Road
   a) Campbell, Robert and Sarah
      i) Robert saw a black Chevrolet on his way to a job (works independently)
      ii) Often sees cars in Amanda's driveway overnight, but he is not certain
      iii) Sarah works in Middlefield at the College; saw nothing unusual that morning
      iv) Couple has lived there for over thirty years
      v) Only see Amanda to speak to; they do not socialize

7) 1514 Old Albany Road
   a) Pierce, John and Amanda
      i) Couple says they know the Griswolds and socialized with them before Frank left
      ii) Now that Amanda is alone, they seldom see her
      iii) Lately, Amanda is not friendly when they do happen to see her

"I struck out at the three of the houses on Amanda's side of the road. The houses are not close and they don't socialize with Amanda much.

"There is a major problem with the witnesses, though; Mary Johnson is adamant about seeing a white car in Amanda's driveway but Robert Campbell says it was black; also, the time they saw the cars is not consistent. I'm afraid that was not much help," Susan concluded.

"Not one of the neighbors who saw the black Chevrolet took the tag number, but then if someone different visits a neighbor's home, one is usually more interested in the person visiting, not how they got there," Richard said.

"Well, it was a good try. I have to get to the morgue for the post-mortem. I don't expect anything unusual, but we need Gordon's opinion as to suicide or murder, which we still don't know. I'll get back as soon as I get James's determination," Karen added.

"I'm going to check with the GBI lab. Marcus said he would put a priority on getting the firearm tested," Richard offered.

"Thank you, Richard.

* * *

After Gordon's post-mortem was completed on Amanda Griswold, Karen returned to the station.

"Welcome back, Karen," Susan greeted.

"Autopsies don't get better with time, Folks. I wish we didn't have to attend them. Anything new while I was gone?"

"I've dug out the ballistics results of the slugs from the Forrester's murders; it's just a hunch, but maybe there is a connection," Richard said.

"What makes you think that?" Susan asked.

"I really can't explain it, Susan, but something is nagging me about it. Maybe the ballistic tests on Griswold's pistol will prove I'm right."

"Shades of Sloan Harrington visions?" Susan teased.

"You know that I don't believe that crap."

"Well, it's a not a bad idea, Richard; maybe you are on to something. James will send the slug he retrieved from Griswold to GBI. It looked to be intact enough to get decent results. However, James says that we should hold our conclusions until the toxicology test results come back from the Lab. There is something bothering James about this death also, but he can't pinpoint it," Karen informed them.

"What does that mean?" Sarah asked.

"There was no evidence of defensive wounds; a single

shot to the head; it makes him suspect that Amanda may have committed suicide. That obviously throws the murder idea into question," Karen responded.

"The cup in the sink dish strainer was clean. It had been washed and left to dry. If it were suicide, why would she do that?" Richard asked.

"That's the same question that James is asking himself."

"If what we are speculating is true, somebody went to quite an effort to stage a murder to appear as a suicide, but why?" Susan added.

"Before the meeting, Marcus called and said that the GBI ballistic test results of the pistol should be here by tomorrow. He has said that he will attend our meeting," Sarah announced.

"That's great. Those results should give us some answers. James confirmed that there were stippling and fouling signs at the entrance site of the bullet wound, so he estimates that the barrel was about two to three inches away from her forehead when it was fired, regardless of who pulled the trigger," Karen explained.

"Most of the suicides that I've investigated, the victim usually puts the muzzle directly against themselves. It seems strange that she would hold it so far away; Doctor Gordon's conclusion doesn't seem right to me," Richard said.

"If we go back to the cup in the dish strainer, what if she was drugged before the person shot her?" Susan probed.

"Couldn't that explain why there were no defensive

wounds?" Sarah asked.

"Well, that is the crux of what is annoying James about this case," Karen said.

"As I said, I attended many suicides by firearms and where the person hasn't blown his head off; most often you find the muzzle stamp at the entrance site, which is usually seen as a stellate or star-shaped wound. Since there was stippling evident, it could mean that her killer held the pistol close to her head.

"Lastly, Karen, I might add that women don't usually off themselves that way. They use drugs, poison, or razor blades, not guns. This case looks more like murder to me. I think we should insist that Doctor Gordon to make a decision here," Richard pushed.

"Come on, Richard, I have too much respect for his skills. He noted the fact that the entrance site was towards the right side of her forehead, above the right eye. We saw that the pistol was found in her lap in her right hand. GBI is doing a gunpowder residue test of swabs from her hand. If that is positive, then he will formally say it was suicide," Karen answered firmly.

"Have we been able to determine anything that would cause Amanda to kill herself?" Susan asked.

"You mean a terminal disease that no one knew about or something like that?"

"No, Doctor Gordon found her to be in very good health. No evidence of anything pathological with major organs, even at her age. He suspects that she could have lived well into her eighties."

"Could it have been some psychological issue that drove her to it?" Sarah asked.

"In my experience talking to her, she was a tough nut; no nonsense and certainly not a person to take any guff from anyone," Karen replied.

"Perhaps we should wait for the GBI fingerprint and ballistic test results before we are at each other's throats," Susan offered.

"There is nothing else that we can do until we know more about the firearm and the toxicology tests. Speculation is not helping us at all," Karen agreed.

Chapter Sixteen

Around noon the following day, the GBI results were received by the MCU. James Gordon agreed to sit in on the meeting to answer any questions that the MCU might have. Karen opened the meeting by displaying the initial report results on the overhead screen.

"In the interest of saving us some time, I have taken the major points out of the report," Karen announced.

1. Firearm identification
    a. Colt, New Frontier
        i. .22 caliber LR
        ii. 4 ¾" model, six shot
        iii. Serial number 23345
        iv. Upon receipt by GBI, confirmed that two bullets had been fired from pistol as reported by MPD (us)
2. Firearm History
    a. Manufacturer sold to an FFL, Andy's Guns, in Seattle, Washington
    b. FFL records show it was sold to Michael K. Damon
    c. MKD now deceased
    d. At present, the sale/trade history of the firearm after the original sale is unknown
3. Fingerprint information
    a. Amanda Griswold's prints found on grip
    b. Two additional smeared fingerprints were evident on the barrel, examination determined they are not useable

4. Ballistic tests (Initial Report)
    a. GBI forensic agent fired four rounds
        i. Bullet characteristics recorded and photographed
    b. Comparison to ballistics examples on file
        i. Test firings then compared to bullet from Forrester murders as requested by the ME (Dr. Gordon)
        ii. Bullet striations match those of the Forrester bullets
        iii. Bullet striations also match those of the Griswold bullet
5. Gunpowder Residue Test on Hands of Mrs. Griswold
    a. Her right hand had significant powder residue
    b. Left hand had no residue
6. Conclusion of GBI Ballistics (Initial Report)
    a. This handgun is the one used in Amanda Griswold's death
    b. The ballistics of this handgun match with the ballistic results of the slugs found at the post-mortems of Marisa and John Forrester

"The ballistic tests by GBI make these cases downright demoralizing, Karen. Now we have three persons killed with the same gun," Richard said.

"Well, I agree. We now know that it is not a coincidence tying these two cases together, but I don't understand yet why it's been so many years apart," Karen replied.

"I don't know the answer to that question, but the same

pistol was used and that means I am correct about Amanda being murdered," Richard interrupted.

"Maybe, Richard, of course, we have no way of knowing when the two bullets were fired; I mean, were they both fired when Amanda died? If so, it could make your position for murder stronger," Karen replied.

"Item 5 of the report shows that she fired the pistol with her right hand. She had powder residue on that hand. That supports the suicide idea…"

"Even so, Susan, it's not conclusive in my mind," Richard interrupted.

"Richard, you should keep in mind that the residue test in not always conclusive. Contact with items such as toilet paper and paper towels could give a false reading. However, we should be confident in this case that the amount of residue most likely shows that she pulled the trigger," Karen advised.

"Yes, Karen, I do know that. Taking all the evidence into account, I am more firmly convinced that Amanda Griswold was murdered. Some of it comes from my calibrated gut, but…"

"Since Green never found the murder weapon, all this time it could have been right next door to the Forresters' house," Sarah speculated.

"To me, that could mean Amanda or Frank Griswold or both conspired to kill the Forresters," Susan ventured.

"That's anyone's guess; Green's interview records show that both Amanda and Frank were interrogated at the time, but they claimed ignorance; he couldn't find any evidence which implicated them.

"We have no information that the two couples were anything more than neighbors. However, Amanda did allude to me that Marisa wasn't as pure as people may have thought. It was easy for me to see that she felt Marisa was after Frank; maybe there was enough motive," Karen answered.

"Well, what was the motive to kill Amanda?" Sarah asked.

"That is the big question; if she was murdered, that is," Karen replied.

"With Amanda dead, we've lost the opportunity from her to determine connections between the Griswold and Forrester families. If there were any connection, she didn't share it with you, Karen," Richard retorted.

"You're right, Richard. She didn't give me any idea that she and her husband were involved in any way with the Forresters, but there was something going on they didn't want known. After all these years, she wasn't ready to admit it. Whatever it was, she protected it until her death," Karen replied.

"It seems to me that the answer to the question of Amanda's suicide or murder is vital to answering that," Richard pushed.

"The problem is that we don't know the gun's history. Anyone could have bought the gun from the original owner, or it may have been given away, lost, or even stolen over the years. I disagree, Richard, even if Amanda was murdered, we would have to find a connection to the present gun owner who may not be her killer," Karen responded.

"Well, then I am out of ideas," Richard said.

"I'll accept that we first need to determine if Amanda was murdered or not," Karen said trying to placate him.

"Do we know if Amanda was right or left handed?" Susan asked.

"That is a great question; her husband would know the answer to that," Karen said.

"Then it is critical now that we question Franklin Griswold. He has been informed of his wife's death. He is making plans to fly out here tomorrow," Susan said.

"As soon as it is decently possible, Susan, I want you to set up an interview with him before he returns to Memphis. Seems that we won't have to make the trip as we had planned," Karen directed.

"Can we check with GBI to see how the residue test came out?" Richard asked.

"I need to call Marcus," Karen answered.

* * *

Marcus Strong was one leader at the GBI whom Karen had developed a strong professional relationship over the years. His support had been pivotal to the solutions of several murder cases that Karen and the MCU had faced. At fifty, Marcus had kept his good looks and physique. He was tall and handsome with a rugged, but pleasant face with a perpetual smile.

"Hi, Marcus, Karen here. I have some questions about the pistol found at the Griswold suicide."

"What makes you believe it is a suicide?" Marcus asked.

"It was my first impression of the scene and Gordon's professional belief that she may have killed herself, but he wasn't certain. We felt it safer from an evidence standpoint if we initially considered her death as a murder until we could prove differently."

"I think that was wise, Karen. As you know, we found her prints on the pistol grip. We were fortunate that it was a wooden one without scrimshaw design so that fingerprints could be taken. However, you knew that there were two spent shells in the cylinder?"

"We didn't, until we received the initial report. We turned the pistol over to you without examining it. I guess that was a little sloppy on our part."

"I'm actually glad your folks didn't handle it; it makes our job a bit easier. I have already spoken to the ballistics lab personnel about it. We received the slug from Gordon's post-mortem of Mrs. Griswold.

"Since you told us that there might be a connection between the Forrester and Griswold death, the ballistic technician went back to cold case evidence room and compared the slugs from the Forrester murders. This is the same pistol was used in their murders also. We noted that in our final report, which is on its way to you," Marcus explained.

"Yes, we are very aware of that; it didn't help us to decide if her death was suicide or not; it simply created more questions," Karen stressed.

"I can't help you there, Karen, but there was some evidence of drug residue in the cup you submitted for chemical tests. It looks as if it could be Rohypnol, but that isn't conclusive at this point."

"Well, well, that pushes us a bit closer to Richard's assertion that she was murdered."

"I'll let you know when we can be certain of the compound," Marcus replied.

"Why the pistol was in Amanda Griswold's possession is something I need to find out. The two spent shells are surprising, though," Karen asserted.

"It looks as though Green may have been chasing the wrong person back then," Marcus interjected.

"Well, something was not right back then. Green's investigation never developed a real suspect. I am glad that I cautioned my MCU folks to consider Griswold's death as a murder not a suicide."

"Again, I think it was a wise move, Karen. If it were murder, the killer may have fired a round first to scare her; then killed her with the second," Marcus answered.

"Thank you, Marcus. I think our precaution about murder vs. suicide was wiser that I originally thought."

"Did your criminalists find any sign of the second slug?"

"No, of course they weren't looking for one. I think that I need to send out the crew again to give a second look at the Griswold home," Karen answered.

"Do you need any help from us?"

"I will let you know if we do. In the meantime, we will go back and scour the place. Thank you."

"Let me know what you find."

* * *

A day later, a .22 caliber slug was found embedded in the door jamb of the doorway leading to the kitchen. It had lodged in such a way as to be nearly invisible. The badly damaged slug was packed and sent to the GBI Lab where it was declared to be of no value to the case in ballistic terms. It was too badly damaged for any forensic usefulness.

* * *

"Good morning, Folks, I should have asked this question earlier, but now it is imperative that we know the answer now. As I told you the other day, we had the 'suicide' pistol with two spent shells in the cylinder supposedly used in Amanda's death. It doesn't mean she didn't try to fire it first at the wall, and then kill herself, but in our interviews, did anyone think to ask her neighbors if she was right or left handed?"

"I think we were all focused to unusual activities which neighbors may have noticed that day," Susan answered.

"Right, and the day I interviewed her, she seemed to use both hands equally when she made coffee and then poured cups for us. Quite frankly, I did not notice," Karen admitted.

"From all the people whom I interviewed on the street, no one seemed to know enough about her, much less about her handedness," Susan said.

"I interviewed the woman at 1509 Old Albany Road. She said that they often had coffee or tea in the morning," Karen volunteered.

"Well, she might know or she may not. I'll give her a call. Otherwise, we did find examples of her handwriting. We should be able to determine her handedness. Sarah has sent the papers to a hand writing expert in Atlanta," Susan added.

At that moment, Sarah entered the room with a report in her hand.

"Good news. I just got Dr. Blain's report by Fax. His opinion, based upon her handwriting, is that she is, rather was, left-handed," Sarah offered.

"That clinches it," Richard said, "She was murdered."

"Well, not quite so fast with the conclusions. The gunpowder residue on her right hand has to be understood. We can't just say that someone else shot her; how do you square it with the residue, Richard?" Susan countered.

"At the moment, I can't, but the feeling is strong that it was murder."

"Also remember, Richard, that we still have to question Frank Griswold. We don't know yet whether he is involved with her death. They weren't exactly playmates for the past decades.

"We need to confirm which was Amanda's dominant

hand. Whoever interviews him should ask that question in a subtle way. He isn't off my radar yet," Karen said with temper.

"So, if he says she was left-handed, that removes any doubt we had?" Richard snorted.

"The bullet hole in her forehead was on the right side and the pistol was found in her right hand. If she was left-handed, it would have been unlikely that she would hold the gun with her right hand. Yes, I think it leads us to the murder scenario," Karen stated.

"Then the questions will be who wanted her dead and why?" Susan mused.

"Finding the connections are frustrating," Sarah voiced.

"By the way, Sarah, how are the financial checks on Amanda Griswold coming along?" Karen asked.

"I've got the past five years only; I don't know if we will be able to go back much farther than that, but there is something very suspicious about her income," Sarah answered.

"What is suspicious?"

"Well, her annual income was quite steady from 2008 to 2010; then it jumped about $500 dollars per month for the past three years."

"What's suspicious about that?" Richard pushed.

"I checked the income sources; her husband or ex, if you prefer, deposits $1000 per month in her checking. Social Security gives her another $800 on the 3rd Wednesday each month."

"So?"

"Let me finish, Richard; the $500 is always deposited in cash exactly one week after her social check comes in."

"And that means?" Richard pursued.

"I think it means that someone was paying her to keep quiet," Sarah replied, "She was blackmailing someone is my guess,"

"I think what you've found is significant; it is probably the reason she was silenced," Karen supplemented.

"What do we do with that now?" Susan wondered out loud.

"It makes your interview with Franklin Griswold that much more important," Karen advised.

Chapter Seventeen

The next morning Susan and Richard went to the Middlefield Hotel to speak with Franklin Griswold.

"Franklin, thank you for agreeing to speak to us at this terrible time. I want to express the sorrow that we all feel for your loss. This is Detective Burnham," Susan said introducing Richard.

"Thank you, Detective, but you know that Amanda and I were separated for many years. I still have feelings for her, but we didn't have too much contact after I left. Too much baggage left behind. She was a hard woman to live with. I suppose she said the same kinds of things about me."

"No, she never voiced that when we interviewed her."

"Why was she interviewed?"

"We reopened the Forrester murder case; she was a witness at the time, so we needed to speak with her."

"Oh, I understand."

"You implied that there was animosity between you two," Susan queried.

"There was a great deal. I never hit her, but the rage was there sometimes. I swear I never touched her in anger."

Listening to him 'swear' to things was no consolation for Susan. He had lied to Green and was probably lying his head off now.

"Why didn't you two divorce?"

"She wouldn't agree to it. You know, married for life

even if we weren't living together. Don't ask me why. I didn't understand it either.

"In a way there was considerable tension. I always resented why she felt she needed to take me back to court for increases in support payments. Just when I would get a raise in pay, she seemed to know, and would get a judge to up the amount. That wasn't right. She could have gotten a job and supported herself."

"When was the last time you spoke to her?"

"I hadn't heard from her for over a year until a week ago. She had called me because she said that she was going to have to speak with one of your detectives and she was nervous about it."

"What was there for her to be anxious about?"

"We knew some things about the Forresters, which they didn't want exposed."

"What kinds of things were those?"

"There were rumors about Marisa having an affair with someone."

"Do you know who that person was?"

"I know Amanda heard that it was me, but that was a lie. I did some work over the years as a neighbor. John was no help around the house, so when a faucet dripped or a fuse blew; she would call me and I would go over and fix it."

"Why would Amanda have believed a rumor that you may have been involved with Marisa?"

"I let slip one time that I thought Marisa was an eyeful, which Amanda took to mean that I wanted to sleep with her. That was totally wrong, but Amanda never trusted me after that. I had to tell Marisa that I couldn't help her anymore. That was part of the reason we eventually split. She just didn't trust me anymore."

"So just for the record, you say that you never slept with Marisa?"

"No, I did not," Franklin shouted.

"Okay, okay, Franklin. How close were you and the Forresters socially beyond your occasional helping her out?"

"We sometimes got together for a barbecue, but that was about it."

"Was John a jealous man?"

"Marisa told both Amanda and me that he could be."

"What does that mean?"

"It means that whenever I helped Marisa and he found out about it he hit the roof. He would shout and threaten her."

"Did he ever physically hurt her?"

"The last time we spoke to her she admitted that he had hit her one time."

"Do you remember the last time that you and Amanda talked to her?"

"I don't remember for sure, but it must have been a few weeks before their murders."

"Do you recall why John was angry enough to hit her?"

"She said that she had told him she was pregnant. She said that John had had a vasectomy three months before.

She thought it was too soon for them to have sex as the doctor had warned them it would not be totally effective for several months and they needed to use other birth control."

"That is very personal information. I am surprised that she shared it with you two."

"You would have to know Marisa. She was very open about things and could give you the wrong impression, if you weren't careful."

"Franklin, I'm not sure I understand about 'the wrong impression.'"

"You know, sometimes you can't be sure whether a woman is giving you the come-on or not."

"Did Marisa give you the 'come-on' during your 'repair' visits?"

"Well, yes, I think that that is what led to the rumor about me and her. It certainly was the reason that Amanda was so unsure about me."

"I'm going to ask again. Did you and Marisa ever have sex?"

"I swear that we didn't," Franklin answered as he turned his head away.

"Look me in the eye, Franklin. Did you and Marisa ever have sex?"

"Okay, okay, we started to, but John had come home for lunch early. I barely had time to get out of the house before he came in. I don't know if she had time to get dressed, but there was yelling as I ran back to my house."

Susan leaned back in her chair, not knowing to what extent he was lying today as he had to Detective Green back then. There was nothing of this revelation in Green's notes, so believing him today was a tremendous stretch.

"Franklin, we have been asking the old neighbors who we are interviewing to give us a DNA swab. Are you willing to do that today?"

"Why do you need that, Detective? Are you saying that I'm a suspect in this case?"

"I know everyone is threatened when asked for a swab, but since you did admit that something happened between you and Marisa; it would be helpful for us to eliminate you as a suspect."

Susan was not about to tell him that their case evidence was spotty at best. Even if he were the father of Marisa's baby, that would not mean that he killed the couple.

"Maybe I should get a lawyer."

"That is your right, but you have not been accused of anything or arrested. You are free to stop speaking with us at any time."

"Let me think about it, I will talk to a lawyer and let you know."

"I still have a few more questions if you are willing."

"Will this take much longer? I have to complete arrangements for Amanda's funeral and get legal things settled about the house."

"That's okay, but access to the house has to wait. At this point, Amanda's death is considered suspicious, and the house can't be disturbed for some time. Sorry, you may have to return to Georgia at a later time."

"When I was told of her death, no one said it was suspicious. I was told that she had to be autopsied, but I didn't understand why. Are you saying that she was murdered?"

"Not necessarily, but do you know of anyone who would want to hurt Amanda?"

"I don't really. Even though she has picked my pocket for the past years, and we stay in legal touch; I don't know her current associates or friends."

"Can we get back to the last time you spoke to Amanda? You said that she was nervous. What would she have been scared about?"

"I don't know if you know this, but Amanda said that she found some things beside Stillwater Creek on the day of the murders."

"Please tell me more."

"Well, she said she found a packet of letters in a leather folder. She opened it and read the letters. She didn't tell me about them for a few days. I wasn't aware of them when Green's detective questioned me."

"What happened when she showed them to you?"

"I read them. They were letters between Marisa and some male. They were love letters."

"Who was the lover?"

"We never found out because they were unsigned."

"Did Amanda think they were your love letters?"

"I couldn't convince her otherwise. I am telling you that it was not me."

"Were there any other kinds of letters in the packet."

"Yes, I believe I saw three threatening letters."

"Where are the letters now?" Susan asked, testing his truthfulness.

"I'm not sure. I made a boxed-in storage place; really it was just an area I opened up in the wall behind the living room bookcase; we stashed the letters there. We promised each other that we would never admit that we had them."

"Amanda said she wasn't sure if there were love letters. She said you took charge of the packet. She told us that there were three hateful letters. She also said that there was a fourth letter. Where are they?"

"I don't remember anything about a fourth letter. I have no idea why she didn't tell you about the love letters. If she had them, she probably put them into the storage area, but I didn't know anything about a fourth letter."

"Did you put the gun there also?"

"What gun?"

"The gun we found in your house. The gun that was found with Amanda."

"Amanda killed herself? How? Why?"

"The first indications are that it was a suicide; the pistol was found in her right hand."

"What? Amanda was left-handed and she wasn't, how do you say it, ambidextrous?"

"You're certain she was left-handed?"

"Positive, in fact, she often complained about having severe cramps in her right hand. In general, as I remember, she didn't have a lot of strength in that hand. I doubt if she could squeeze the trigger of a gun."

"Again, what do you know about the gun we found?"

"I don't know about any gun, I swear."

"Did you ever own a .22 caliber pistol?"

"I did years ago; I met a guy on the train to Memphis one time when I was traveling and sold it to him."

"Will you take us to your storage place in the living room?"

"I thought I couldn't go to the house?"

"You can go with us."

"Yes, if it will help you to see I had nothing to do with this mess."

* * *

Griswold accompanied by Susan and Richard went to the house.

"Okay, Franklin, please show us where you and Amanda placed the letters."

Franklin went to the built-in bookcase. On the third shelf, he pulled out a large dictionary and a large Bible, which were situated against the bookcase left wall.

Behind the now absent book spaces, Susan and Richard could barely see a makeshift door, which blended well with the back wall. Franklin then pushed on the right lower corner of the door, which slid open showing a space that had been burrowed out of the wall. Richard took a flashlight and streamed it into the void. It was empty.

"Franklin, who else knew of this hiding place?"

"Only Amanda and me; I swear."

"I have to clear something up, Franklin; Amanda recently told Major Hunter that she had seen a white car leaving the Forresters' house the day of the murder. Did she tell you about it?"

"She never told me about any white car. If she had, I would have probably told her to keep her mouth shut and not get involved."

"Don't you think that if a person has knowledge of a crime detail, they should tell the police?"

"I do not think that at all. It usually only gets the person into trouble even though they may be innocent."

"It's a strange way to look at things, Franklin," Richard asserted.

"Franklin, we have uncovered something puzzling about Amanda's finances," Susan added.

"I pay my support to her every month; I haven't missed a payment in years, so don't try to pin something on me."

"We are well aware about your punctual payments; no, that isn't the problem; what we have found is that Amanda was receiving $500 dollars in cash each month for the past three years. Do you have any idea who could be paying her that kind of money?"

"I don't believe it! Maybe she's working the corners of Middlefield; how the hell should I know?"

"Come on, Franklin, get serious; this may give a clue as

to who may have seen her last. I am not playing some sort of game with you. Do you have any idea who might have been paying her this money?"

"I really don't; Amanda had always been somewhat secretive during our marriage, but it could be a sugar daddy or she has something on someone."

"Did she ever mention anything to you that may lead us to this person?"

"I really haven't a clue. Not really, wait; she said one time that 'people pay dearly to protect those that they love.' I asked her what she meant, but she just shrugged her shoulders; there was never any more talk of that."

"One last question, Franklin; who do you suppose was Marisa's lover?" Susan queried.

"Honestly, I don't know."

"Okay, would you be willing to give us a DNA swab today?"

"No, I still want to talk to a lawyer first. I don't want to give you a swab until then. As much as I would like to clear my name, I think that you are just looking to pin the Forrester murders on me."

"Are you sure you want to do this?"

"Yes."

"We can get a warrant if you persist with this refusal," Susan pushed.

"Then I suggest you do that. Am I under arrest?"

"No, you are free to go. Thank you for your help, Franklin," Susan said.

After Griswold left, Susan and Richard met with Karen to start the process for a court ordered DNA swab from Franklin Griswold.

* * *

"What reason did Judge Smalls give for refusing the order?" Richard asked unbelievingly.

"He said that there was not enough probable cause to issue the order against Griswold."

"Is he willing to reconsider?"

"No, we need to remember him come election time," Susan said.

"Better than that, we have to get some political pressure to have him sign Griswold's order."

Three days later, they had their DNA court order.

Chapter Eighteen

The area of Jacksonville that Richard had envisioned was not what he found. The Golden Oaks subdivision was one of several, which had sprung up in the late '90s. Its gated entry signaled that this was a place of refuge not to be disrupted by just anyone seeking entrance.

It was evident that this community represented those with sufficient means. They had achieved success in their lives and had chosen to reside there.

Approaching the gate, Richard strained to peer into the interior, but his view was blocked as the roadway beyond the entry gate which abruptly made a sharp turn hindering vision of what lay ahead.

A stout, uniformed gate guard approached Richard's car from the security base and inquired as to his business.

"Good morning, Sir; may I help you?"

Richard observed the nametag on her uniform.

"Good morning, Mary; I am Detective Burnham of the Middlefield, Georgia Police Department. I'm here to see Mister Randolph F. Williams," Richard said while displaying his identification and badge.

The guard eyed Richard's badge as though this was the first time she had ever seen one.

"Thank you, Mister Burnham; just a moment please."

Then with a somewhat graceful circle, she dutifully returned to her station and immediately reached for the telephone. Richard watched as she dialed some number while periodically turning to face him. When she reached the recipient of her call, she gestured several times, the meaning of which Richard could only guess, before concluding the call.

"Apparently, Mister Williams is not expecting you this morning," she said sweetly.

"I understand; would you please call him back and inform him that I am accompanied by Officer James Smith of the Jacksonville Police. We do need to speak with him this morning," Richard retorted.

"Very good, Sir; I will call him."

"James, this a bit strange; the person I am here to interview was never what I would call a success in life. This place seems out of reach for someone like him. This is not what I expected; I thought we would find him living in a run-down trailer. This surprises me," Richard voiced with some consternation.

"According to our information, he has lived here for ten years; he was one of the original occupants. Perhaps he married well, or hit the lottery," Smith replied.

"Yeah, possibly, we'll have to see."

When the guard returned to the car, Richard asked, "Can you give me directions to his residence?"

"It is 4235 White Oak Lane; it will be the third left on the main access road," she replied while lifting the barrier.

The drive to White Oak Lane wound its way past several streets and many speed bumps.

"This development is huge," Richard uttered with some

amazement.

"I've only been here one other time," Smith replied, "And that was a call for a minor domestic dispute. This development has given us very few problems over its ten-year existence. It is a beacon for those with money."

"I can see why; the houses are small castles. No doubt wealth lives here."

"Yes, some well-known names reside here."

Nearing Williams address, Richard saw tennis courts and the all-important swimming pool that Olympic contenders would prize.

"Looks as though they could sponsor their own swim teams," Richard said with some admiration.

Reaching the address, Richard exited the car; taking several moments to let the impact of what he saw fix solidly in his mind. Then he and Smith approached the house; cautious of what may await them.

The house was huge; Richard estimated that it must be over fourteen thousand square feet sitting on some three acres. The building itself was comprised of two floors with two tall chimneys symmetrically placed on each side of the massive roof.

Wide terraces on each floor swept around the front of the home and along both sides furnishing convenience for the occupants. Large, full length windows and multiple sliding glass doors provided access and attractive displays overlooking manicured gardens and neatly clipped lawns.

A separate building provided space for automobiles,

which Burnham and Smith noted had room for seven lucky cars parked at an angle within the great structure.

"This makes my home look absolutely rustic," Richard thought, "This must have cost a fortune, even ten years ago."

Approaching the entrance which was located beneath the spacious veranda, Richard rapped the heavy, brass entry door knocker featuring a great lion's head holding a solid brass ring in its mouth.

The door was opened by a uniformed man who asked them the purpose of their visit. After displaying their identifications, he directed them into the library to await Randy Williams.

Within five minutes, a tall man immaculately dressed in a suit with waistcoat approached them with an outstretched hand.

"Good morning, Gentlemen, what is the nature of this unexpected visit?"

"Mister Randolph Williams?" Richard asked.

"I am; how can I help you?"

"We need to ask you a few questions concerning an unsolved murder case we have in Georgia."

"Murder case? What would I have to do with that?" the man questioned.

"When did you last live in Georgia?"

"I have never lived in Georgia, Sir. I moved from Colorado ten years ago after retiring. I sold my business and decided to move to warmer climate."

"What was the nature of your business?" Richard asked.

"What difference does it make to you? What is this all about?" Williams retorted.

"I don't know if it makes a difference, but for the record I need to know."

"If you must know, the business was 'Williams Precious Metals,' which owned a working gold mine."

"I need to clarify something. Are you Randolph Francis Williams?" Richard asked.

"No, I am Randolph Stanley Williams."

Realizing their mistake, Richard apologized, "I am sorry for the mix-up, Mister Williams; the man we wish to question is Randolph F. Williams. Again, I am terribly sorry for the confusion."

"I'll accept your apology, but I can understand. There is another Randolph Williams living here in Jacksonville. His mail is sometimes delivered here; it's a damn nuisance."

"We won't take up any more of your time Mister Williams. We will be going."

"Robert will show you out."

"Thank you," Richard replied and immediately left.

* * *

"I'm sorry, James, that was an embarrassing mess," Richard said as they drove away, "Someone in our office screwed up on the middle name."

"It happens; let's go to the station and find the correct guy," Smith replied.

Back at the Jacksonville base, the address for Randolph

203

Francis Williams was located and verified. Other officers at the station had a good laugh at the discomfort of Richard and James having accosted one of the finest citizens of Jacksonville.

Before they departed, Smith warned Richard that the station had much experience with that particular trailer park. Late night drunken brawls and domestic fighting were the most common cause for police involvement.

After the humiliating mistake of the last visit, the trailer park, which Richard and James now approached was more in line with what Richard had envisioned for Randy Williams. He was somewhat surprised that the mobile homes were slightly above average condition compared to those he had seen in similar parks over the years.

"James, this park is not what I expected. Your comment about the problems the department faces…"

"I know, but alcohol makes people do bad things regardless of what kinds of houses they live in."

A few of the trailer homes located towards the back of the park were in dire need of maintenance having sun faded paint, broken window screens, and stairs in such condition that they would not support the smallest child.

"Where are the building inspectors," Richard thought.

Many homes showed efforts at garden plantings around the dwellings to make the dismal surroundings a somewhat pleasant setting, but the attempts were not successful.

The roads into and out of the park were not the boggy graveled ruts he had seen in his travels as a detective, but they were not much better.

As Richard drove further into the park, James, directed him to Greenview Road where Williams lived. Along the way, they saw children playing in a field. Realizing that the central location of the bank of mailboxes would not help to locate Williams' trailer, he stopped the car and asked directions from a young boy.

"Where is the Williams trailer," Richard asked in his politest police tone of voice.

"Who wants to know?" came the sassy reply.

"The Police want to know," Richard answered.

"What do want you with him?"

"We need to talk to him," Richard replied with some impatience in his voice.

"It's right down the road; two more trailers and you're there," the boy responded.

"Come over here," Richard commanded the boy.

When the child reached the car, Richard handed him a dollar for his help, but it was refused.

"My mother says I can't take things from a stranger," he replied.

"You have a very smart mother. What is your name?"

"Jason."

"Jason what?"

"Jason Williams."

"Is Randy Williams your father?"

"Yes."

Parked next to Williams's home was a black Chevy

Impala about five or six years old. Richard made a mental note for use later while he and Smith approached the door.

Introducing himself, he could see the shift in the man's countenance when he realized who was there, but he welcomed them in and offered coffee. Sensing no hostile situation, the two entered the trailer.

Richard surveyed the interior of the trailer, noting that it had the stamp of a bachelor. The best he could describe it was an "ordered mess."

While the man was preparing the coffee, Richard made small talk while trying to appraise the person he had come to investigate.

Randy Williams was, he judged, to be in his mid-sixties and appeared to be in good health. He stood six feet tall with a solid frame developed over the years from hard work. He had brown eyes and hair restrained in a gray pony-tail containing remnants of brown color, even at this stage of his life.

Williams demeanor was placid and non-threatening. Richard wondered if his behavior would last through the interview. Anna Smithson had told Susan that Williams suffered from blackouts when under stress, which Williams would swear he could not remember. She had mentioned that Randy could be violent during these times.

"Mister Williams, I met a lad outside who says his name is Jason Williams and that you are his dad."

"Call me Randy. Nah, he doesn't know who his father is. He has his mother's last name. She is a sweet kid who got into trouble and had Jason. The guy left town.

"He has no one to look up to. Jason spends quite a bit of time with me. I guess I'm the father figure he needs. He just uses my last name. I don't mind. I take him fishing and we go to the movies, sometimes his mother comes with us.

"I've been helping him and his mother out for a few years. I buy them groceries or take them shopping when they need. The rumors fly around here that I really am Jason's father, but that is bunk.

"I never had kids when I was married. No, he's not my true son, but he and I act as though he is. It's good for me and him. I'm not saying that I'm such a good guy, but the kid does need someone he can talk to other than his mother. Of course, I have to tell his mother now and then to act more responsibly. Alcohol makes her forget what she should stop doing, if you know what I mean."

"Randy, I would like to ask you a few questions to help us with a case."

"What case is that?"

"It's the Forresters' murder case; it has been re-opened. We know that you were at their residence on the day of their murders. I wanted to take you back to that day and understand what you may have witnessed."

"That day has remained in my memory all these years. As I think I told the detective back then; I went for my last pay; I never got it. When I went onto the porch, I heard shouting from inside the house; I ran to the barn and left when Anna came to pick me up."

"Do you know who was in the house?"

"I have no idea who it was. There were angry voices. I thought I could hear Marisa sobbing, but I wasn't sure. Other than that I didn't see anyone or anything."

"So you are saying that you did not enter the house at all that day?"

"I am definitely saying that. You can ask Anna, if you don't believe me."

"But you said that Anna wasn't there when you went onto the porch?"

"Yes."

Richard knew that Green's interview notes of Williams were still being sought. For whatever reason, that binder had been misplaced.

"We've spoken to your ex-wife and she told us her memory of that morning's events."

"I see. Anna was always so helpful."

"Her version is that she drove you to the Griswold house around ten a.m., so that you could finish up some work. Apparently you had worked your last day for the Forresters the week before because they had fired you. You were going to their house that day to get your pay and settle something with John Forrester. Is that true?"

"Yes, Anna told you the truth."

"What happened for them to fire you?"

"Marisa didn't fire me; it was John. Three months earlier, Marisa had asked me to come to the house to help her get some things down from the attic. While we were up there, Marisa had pointed to a tall shelf, which held two old suitcases.

"I asked her why she needed them and she said that she needed to pack some things for travel. I didn't realize it until later, but she may have been packing up to leave John.

"Since I was much taller, I stood behind her as she tried to reach them and our bodies touched in an intimate way. She did not object, but just then John appeared at the stairway and began screaming at us. We both tried to explain it was not what it seemed. He told me to get out and never come back. As I was leaving, I could hear him threatening Marisa."

"You said that this happened three months earlier, so why did you go back the day of the murders?"

"As I said, he fired me, not Marisa, so I kept working. I made sure to be around the house only when John was not at home."

"I have to ask, were you and Marisa intimate?"

"I am ashamed to admit it. I know Anna suspected it, but I swear it was only once. It was shortly after the attic incident. Somehow Anna realized what must have happened between Marisa and me. When I finally confessed to her, she was furious but she agreed to give me a second chance. We made plans to leave the area for Colorado to start a new life as soon as we could save up enough money. I was afraid that the police would try to pin the murders on me, so Anna agreed to the move."

"What happened in Colorado with your marriage? Did

you stay true to her?"

"I tried; honestly I did. I did love Anna and wanted to stay together."

"Was your infidelity with Marisa the primary cause of your divorce?"

"In many ways, yes, Anna never got over it. Eventually she wanted a divorce even though I stayed true to her."

"Did Anna ever write any letters to Marisa?"

"She may have; I really don't know."

"Was Anna just angry with you about Marisa, or was she also angry at her?"

"She did tell me once that she hated her for what she had done."

"So that may be the reason, Anna Smithson wouldn't outright admit to Susan about Randy's infidelity with Marisa," Richard thought. "I wonder if she acted on her hate?"

"That day when I went to Marisa's home was only to pick up my pay. As I said before, I never saw her or John because of the ruckus going on in the house. When I heard Anna arriving to pick me up. I ran from the barn to the car and we left. I swear that is the truth."

"What was the car you owned at the time?"

"It was a 1970 white Chevy Monte Carlo. I loved that car."

"Very interesting," Richard thought. "Must check this out."

"Even though the car was nine years old at the time, it

ran like a top; I changed the oil and filter every three thousand miles; it had over one hundred ninety thousand miles on it before I got rid of it."

"Anna said that your truck was in the garage that day for service. Is that true?"

"Yes."

"I understand that you were the handyman for several other neighbors in that area of Old Albany Road."

"Yes, I worked for many people along that road."

"I'll get to the point. A woman for whom you did some work years ago was found dead a few weeks ago. Her death seems mysterious; you may be able to answer a few things about her."

"Who are you talking about?"

"Amanda Griswold."

"Amanda Griswold? Amanda Griswold and Frank were two of my best customers. That is sad; I had heard about it. Did you catch the person yet?"

Richard's next breath stopped short, "What had he heard?" he asked himself.

"What makes you think there is 'a person to catch?' " Richard asked.

"I guess I heard it on the news."

Richard made a note and decided to move on. He would discuss this with the MCU folks when he returned to the station.

"When did you last speak to Amanda or Frank?"

"I haven't seen or talked to Amanda or Frank in years."

"I have to ask if you were in the Stillwater area on Tuesday the fifteenth."

"Um, let's see, I did have to make a trip to Macon somewhere around that time. I have an old friend who lives there. We get together now and then."

"Would he be able to verify that?"

"He wouldn't be able to verify anything because he is not a he; he is a she."

"Please give me her name so we can check that."

"This is very sensitive, Detective, you see she is married and I wouldn't want her husband to find out that we get together. There's nothing bad about this, it's just that he gets jealous."

"So you just meet and have coffee?"

"Yeah, something like that."

Richard thought to himself, "Right, I'm sure it's just coffee. You haven't changed, Randy."

"Well, you should give me her name. If you have her phone number, we will be discreet with our questions to her."

"Am I a suspect or something? I don't see why I have to prove where I was a couple of weeks ago. This is still a free country, isn't it?"

"Amanda Griswold's death is suspicious. I can't say anything more about it right now, but we want to check out any present and old acquaintances. So, unfortunately I have to ask these things. I wish I didn't."

"Her name is Mary Parsons. Her husband is a big-wig

in Lizella politics."

"I thought you said she was in Macon."

"I wasn't honest, Detective. I really don't want you to contact her."

"Randy, don't be foolish. We have to clear these things up. You certainly know the process from the Forresters' murders. It has to be done. Give me the phone number."

Williams complied and Richard wrote it down on the pad he always carried.

"Is there anything else you would like to tell me about the Forresters or the Griswolds?"

"I said that Amanda and Frank Griswold were among my best customers. That is true, but they were also good friends. Anna and I visited them often. They were kind to us. We never had much money; they often had us over for supper. That's the kind of people they were."

"Were they also friends with the Forresters?"

"They were. Both often talked about the family and kids. Frank and Amanda always wanted kids, but it never happened."

"So their relationship with the Forresters was just that, friends?"

"As far as I know, yes. Marisa said one time that sometimes she was uncomfortable around Frank, but she didn't really say why."

"Anna said that you owned an old pickup truck?"

"Yes, I bought it from some guy earlier in the year. There was an ad in the paper. I met some woman and paid her one hundred bucks for it. She said her husband owned the truck, but he couldn't be there, so she had to meet me and make the sale.

"It was an old one with many miles on it. It was my first truck."

"Did the woman give you the title?"

"No, she didn't have one; she said her husband just wanted to get rid of it. No title. I wasn't sure if I was buying a stolen truck or not.

"At the time, I didn't have the money to get tags for it. Later I drove it to Jacksonville and got Florida plates. I had a friend in Florida who helped to get me a title and tags for it.

"After I got it registered, I usually drove it to my jobs, but I think it wasn't available that day."

"What was the color of this truck?"

"I think it was green."

"It wasn't 'baby-blue?' "

"Are you kidding me? I wouldn't get caught dead in a truck that color."

"How long did you keep that truck?"

"When we started our move to Colorado, I drove it; Anna drove our car. The truck died halfway there; it was too expensive to fix, so it wound up in a junkyard."

"That about wraps up my questions for today, Randy. I may need to contact you again if I have forgotten something. Thank you."

"I hope you catch whoever did it," Randy offered as they

parted.

Richard kept his poker face, but wondered how Randy knew. Nothing about how Amanda had died was released to the press.

"Why did you say 'I hope you catch whoever did it?' "

"Well, didn't you say her death was suspicious?"

"I did; please remember that suspicious can mean many things, Randy."

When Richard reached the car, he called Karen with Mary Parson's phone number; asking her to call Parsons to check out Williams' alibi.

"Let's see how truthful Randy is," Richard said.

Chapter Nineteen

The next morning, Richard, Karen and Susan met to discuss Williams' interview.

"How did the interview work out, Richard?" Karen asked.

"A few things he said are puzzling. For one, when I brought up Amanda's death, he asked, 'Did you catch the person yet?' "

"Hmm. How did he know that?"

"I may have made the mistake of calling her death suspicious."

"Not good, but okay, what else?"

"Secondly, when I asked about a pickup truck he bought from a woman's husband, he told me that it was green in color, not blue."

"If Amanda was right, the truck leaving that she saw was blue; was she lying to us?" Karen speculated.

"Who knows? I can chalk some of this ambiguity to fading memories, but something is smelly about these interviews."

"Yes, our 'witnesses' are hiding things, and not very well, I might add."

"On the other hand, Karen, didn't Amanda say that she saw a white car leaving before the mailman arrived?"

"She certainly did. What are you thinking?"

"According to Williams, his wife dropped him off at the Griswolds and picked him up at Forrester's house. Their

216

car was a white Chevy Monte Carlo, 1970. If she is not lying, the car she saw leaving could have been Williams' car, but the truck story doesn't fit very well with Evan's story. What was she up to?"

"Evans must not have seen the car because he said that he saw a truck driving away that was blue, baby-blue," Karen added.

"Both Anna Smithson and Randy said the truck he bought was green," Richard responded.

"Something is definitely not right here. It may not be anything we can resolve after all these years. What else?"

"Randy admitted that he and Marisa had sex; only once, he claimed, about three months before her death."

"Did he say that he told Anna?"

"He said that he admitted it to her. She apparently went ballistic; he said that she gave him a second chance. The requirement was that they move away from the area. Eventually they went to Colorado."

"I wonder if her anger spilled over to Marisa?"

"I thought that also. He said he wasn't sure if she ever wrote any letters to Marisa, but he said that Anna may have hated her for that."

"Did he know about Marisa's pregnancy?"

"I didn't ask; he didn't mention it, but I think that she may have told him."

"That's a bit sloppy on our part, Richard. Her pregnancy is a major piece of our thinking. It goes to a possible motive."

"You're right, it was. That's just a guess on my part, however, if Marisa thought Williams was the father she probably would have told him. It's possible, but somehow I doubt it. It would have complicated her marriage even more. Now that you mention it, Karen, I wonder if Anna knew about Marisa's pregnancy?"

"I wonder if Amanda knew about it? That may help explain a few things."

"From what we have learned, both Anna and Amanda may have had a reason to hold a grudge," Richard uttered.

"This case is getting messier and messier. There is no record of Green interviewing Anna Williams unless it is in the missing binder with Randy's."

"If he didn't interview her at the time, Karen, we have spotted another hole in his approach."

"I am becoming painfully aware of his short comings in this. I hate to admit that Green was slipping."

"Well, it's history, Karen, someday someone may criticize what we are doing."

"Right. Did you ask if he would give us a swab?"

"I didn't. I told him we may have more questions in the future and to let us know if he was leaving the area."

"What really bothers me is that he seems to know more about how Amanda died than was in the papers," Karen said.

"That's true, but remember I had said that her death was suspicious, so he may have assumed it was foul play."

"We have to follow up on that. As far as his alibi is

concerned, this Parson woman couldn't remember exactly which day she had spent time with Williams. Her account is that it was either the day before the date of Amanda's death or after; she just couldn't remember. I could tell that she really didn't want to admit she was seeing Williams."

"Well, I can understand that. It puts her world in jeopardy."

"I think we have to have a swab from Williams. Judge Smalls signed the order."

"I'll ask the Jacksonville police to take one. I spoke to the Chief down there and told him we might be making a request in the future."

"Good, I'll have Sarah fax the order to him."

"Karen, I suggest that we have a quick review of the information we have on Evans, Williams, and Griswold. All three were involved in one way or another with the Forresters," Richard recommended.

"Well, how are you going to tie one of them to the Forresters' murders, Richard?"

"Right now, I don't know."

"We have Amanda Griswold's murder to solve here and now; in my mind that takes precedence over the Forresters. The Chief and the Mayor will start pressing before long. The *Patriot* has been getting pushy for details; I can't ignore them much longer," Karen insisted.

"You've been pretty quiet this morning, Susan, what do you think?" Richard asked.

"I agree that Amanda's murder takes precedence, Karen,

219

but perhaps there is a connection between the three murders," Susan said forcefully.

"Are you suggesting that Frank Griswold killed his estranged wife?"

"I don't know what to believe yet, but yes, it is possible."

"I recommend that we try to sort out the confusing things we have learned as a result of the interviews," Richard pushed.

"Let's break for lunch and the meet at two to continue this. Call Sarah and ask her to join us then."

* * *

Karen opened the meeting by announcing, "From earlier discussions with each of you, we believe the probable suspects for the Griswold murder are: Williams, Evans, and Frank Griswold. Each had the opportunity to get to Middlefield on the day of Amanda Griswold's murder; each may have had a reason to kill her."

"The question is, what was the motive?" Susan quizzed.

"Amanda must have had information that points to one of them, and decided to extort some money. From her bank records, she wasn't greedy for the big take, but a monthly stipend would do," Richard added.

"The problem is that my interview with Amanda didn't give us any hints. Yes, she lied years ago to Green's guys, but she gave me no indication that either she or Frank was somehow involved with Marisa other than socially. Wait, I take that back; she did give me a sense of jealously about

Frank having to do little jobs for Marisa."

"What if our killer back then was actually Amanda?" Susan interjected.

"It certainly seems possible. What if the father of Marisa's baby was Frank and Amanda knew about it?"

"That is motive enough in my book," Richard said, "Further, the killings of the Forresters were done with a woman's weapon."

"Richard, what are you talking about, a woman's weapon? Is it the knife? The pistol?"

"Both." Richard answered.

"I admit she could have easily handled the .22 caliber pistol, but I'm not sure that clinches the argument," Karen said.

"What if Frank's DNA proves he was the father?" Susan asked.

"Well, even if true; it doesn't necessarily follow that Amanda killed them. It would take an uncontrollable anger to kill both John and Marisa. She didn't impress me that way," Karen exhorted.

"Come on, Karen, thirty years is a long time to cool off," Richard said with some anger.

"Also, Karen, isn't it strange that it was Amanda who found those 'incriminating letters' in a folder beside Stillwater Creek? Just good luck I suppose," Susan added.

"What if she is the one who wrote them," said Richard with some smugness in his voice.

"Well, wouldn't Frank have recognized Amanda's

handwriting?" Karen said.

"What about the love letters? Wouldn't Amanda have recognized Frank's handwriting if he wrote them?" Susan retorted.

"I admit that your points are possible, but what do we do with that now?" Karen asked expecting no answers.

"I believe that if Frank is proven to be the father, we lean on him and I mean hard," Richard said.

"What will that do for us?" Susan asked.

"I understand what Richard is saying. If Amanda was the killer and Frank knew that she was; he became an accessory to two murders by not telling Green," Karen agreed.

"If she were the killer, she could have kept the pistol and put it in their safe place," Susan added.

"I'm sorry, Karen, this is a silly question, but did Amanda say when they built the 'safe place'?" Sarah asked.

"Frank said that he built it right after Amanda found the letters," Susan responded.

"I guess that I am agreeing with Susan that if Amanda were the killer, she, rather, they needed to hide them," Sarah stated.

"If Amanda were the killer, I can't understand why, after all these years, she would suddenly want to bring the letters to us. She must have known that it would eventually lead to some difficult questions," Karen exclaimed.

"What if the killer were Frank? A motive to kill Amanda

could have been blackmail," said Richard.

"You think that she was blackmailing Frank, her own husband?" Sarah asked, disbelieving the idea.

"It is possible. They weren't exactly lovebirds at this point."

"Also, Frank said that Amanda was always asking for more money for support. If he thought that she was the killer, why didn't he go to the police with his suspicion?" Susan ventured.

"This speculation is making me very uncomfortable. All of it is possible, I suppose, but worse, it doesn't really get us any closer to her killer. We could wind up with egg on our face," Karen said with frustration.

"It would be a help to know if Frank's the father. If he were, we have a toe in the water, but that is about all. I have no doubt that the Griswolds were involved in some way. The story Amanda finally told you, Karen, was to make her seem an innocent while making Frank look as though he had a motive to kill the Forresters," Richard said.

"I admit she dropped enough innuendo to try to convince me that Frank may have been involved with Marisa."

"A more intriguing question is where was the murder weapon hidden all these years," Susan pushed.

"If we knew that, we would know who the killer is."

"It has to be Frank; who else could it be? He killed the Forresters; Frank then killed Amanda to keep her quiet," Susan said smugly.

"And his reason for killing them is?" Karen retorted.

"The baby, the baby, the baby," Susan nearly shouted.

"If you're right, Susan, we have to break his story. Memphis is not so far away that he couldn't drive here; kill Amanda, and return home," Richard interrupted.

"Why would he kill her after all these years?" Sarah asked.

"She was blackmailing him; she thought he killed the Forresters; she suspected he was the father of Marisa's baby; that's why they never divorced; the truth would come out.

"The final straw for Frank was that she answered our ad in the paper; he knew she would eventually break after all these years," Susan said pushing her theory.

"I still can't believe that a wife would try to blackmail her husband," Sarah said.

"I don't mean to be condescending, Sarah, but you are new to this game and unmarried. For a myriad of reasons, blackmail and murder happens between married couples, especially estranged couples," Richard said smugly.

"It is still hard to believe..."

"What is the color of his car?" Karen asked to end the escalating tension.

"He has a 2011 Ford Explorer and a 2009 Chevrolet Impala registered to him; both black," Sarah answered.

"I think we should arrest him," Richard nearly shouted.

"Calm down, Richard, we have no proof. Yes, we should interrogate him; I mean really put the screws to him, but unless something else pops up, we can't arrest him; we have no proof unless we can get a credit card trail from Memphis to here around the time Amanda was killed. Even with that, it doesn't necessarily mean he killed her," Karen declared.

"I'll get right on it, Karen," Sarah said starting to leave the room.

"Hang on a minute, Sarah," Karen directed.

"Susan, you said 'the baby' three times. At this point, we don't know if it was John Forrester's or not. At least let's find out if one of the three guys we suspect was the father of Marisa's baby. Then maybe we can stop arguing about things that are just speculation," Richard angrily exclaimed.

"What do you suggest if none of them turn out to be the father?" Karen asked.

"In that case, I don't know what we do next," Richard responded.

"Honestly, I am beginning to despair. Green must have felt this way; this effort is hopeless," Susan said.

"Okay, Sarah, follow up with Jacksonville, Memphis, and Orlando departments. We have to have those swabs. I will call the DNA lab and ask for them to prioritize our tests. Also, check what Evans and Williams have for vehicles registered in their names. In the meantime, I need a break. We meet tomorrow at ten."

Chapter Twenty

"Sarah, have the swabs been taken?" Karen inquired.

"Yes, Evans and Griswold's were obtained yesterday afternoon. Williams's will be taken today."

"Good, I will call Marcus to make certain they are expedited at the GBI lab."

"Can I ask why we are meeting today? We don't have the auto information and the DNA results yet," Richard pushed.

"We are meeting because I want to let the Forrester work rest for now. I want us to focus on other factors about Amanda's murder," Karen answered.

"And what would those 'factors' be, Karen?" Richard questioned.

"We've talked about motive and gone around in circles trying to justify our belief that Frank and Amanda somehow were involved in the Forresters' deaths. Now let's discuss possible motives for Williams or Evans to have killed Amanda."

"If we were correct in assuming that Frank had a motive because of Amanda blackmailing him; couldn't she have done the same to one of the other two?" Susan asked.

"If Williams murdered Marisa, he would have blood splattered on him from the stabbings, but Anna Smithson made no mention of blood on him when she picked him up that day." Karen recounted.

"You said that she said he came from the barn with his

tools in a satchel. Couldn't he have changed his clothing before she picked him up?" Richard asked.

"Let me see," Susan said rechecking her notes. "Yes, she said he came running to the truck from the barn."

"So my thought is that he may have killed them and Anna wouldn't have seen any blood on him, or was she lying?"

"She did say that Williams was very upset. That could have been because he just killed two people or had found the two dead. Unless he confesses to us, we will never know. She said that he never confessed to her," Susan added.

"He could have put his bloody clothes into his tool bag along with the gun. He could have carried an extra set of work clothes. Anna would have never known," Richard said.

"You're saying that Anna would not have noticed his different set of clothes from the morning?" Karen said disbelievingly.

"Richard, of course a wife would know if her husband had on different clothes. If you ever come home dressed differently; Aretha will know; take it from me," Susan said with great emphasis.

"Okay, okay; I still think it could have happened," Richard pushed.

"So, you're saying that Williams pre-meditated the murders," Karen interrupted.

"If he were the father of the baby, then he had a motive,"

Richard smugly responded.

"Possible, possible, Richard. What about Evans?"

"I ruled him out because he had a schedule to meet, you know, the mail delivery. I can't see the timing necessary for him to commit the murders and still continue his route."

"But he didn't finish his route that day; Green didn't finish interviewing him until late in the day," Susan said.

"Did Green or his detectives ever check Evan's mail van?"

"I don't believe there is any reference in the interview report," Richard responded.

"That is something we need to go back to the records and check," Karen directed.

"After this meeting, I will do that, Karen," Richard volunteered.

"Again, if Evans did this, it would have been pre-meditated."

"Why would it have to be, Karen?"

"His rushing in to sweep up the kids may have been an act of humanity, but it could have been a way to get blood on himself, which would not be questioned."

"Hindsight is great. I suppose that we could castigate Green for not seeing this at the time," Richard said.

"I'm not suggesting that, Richard. Looking at this case thirty plus years does give us an advantage in a way. We can ask questions that may have been lost in the excitement of the time. That's all," Karen explained.

"Okay, but what would be Evan's motive?"

"Couldn't the motive have been the same as Williams's if he were the father?" Susan speculated.

"Of course, but the question is would it have been enough to make him kill two people? It just doesn't make sense to me," Karen responded.

"You can make the same argument for each of the three," Richard interrupted.

"I agree with Karen. Marisa was not a loose woman as far as we can tell. She appears to have been in a loveless marriage and may have weakened when someone came along at the right time. She and this person may have fallen in love. I can't see a reason Evans would have killed her if he were the one. Also, he was in a secure job and in a happy marriage with children," Susan defended.

"I agree with you and Karen on that. I believe Williams is the most likely one; the other two had good jobs and were settled in their lives. As for Williams, he was really a vagabond worker and because of what Anna said about his having a liberal attitude toward extra-marital sex separates him from the other two," Sarah said.

"Well, if Williams turns out not to be the father, then that goes out the window," Richard said.

"Okay, okay, Folks. We've swung back to the baby thing again. I really wanted to discuss what opportunities and motives 'our' three would have for killing Amanda.

"What about the opportunity for Evans or Williams to get to town and kill Amanda?" Karen asked.

"Right, they each live within drivable distances, Karen,"

Richard said.

"I asked last week for us to check credit card records for each of them. Can we have a report about that?"

"I checked records for the past six months for each of them," Sarah answered.

"Why six months, Sarah?" Susan asked.

"I wanted to see any patterns in their travel. Of the three, Williams actually travels the most. He made nine trips to New England since the first of the year, and fourteen to Georgia in the past two months."

"Where in Georgia?"

"Middlefield nine times and Atlanta the rest."

"Was he here when Amanda was murdered?" Susan asked.

"In fact, he was. He arrived in Middlefield two days before Amanda's murder and left the next day back to Florida."

"Did Williams tell you he travels to our area?" Karen asked Richard.

"He did; I noted that in my interview report."

"Hmm, I didn't focus on that as I should have, Richard. I did tell you all that Williams' alibi wasn't that solid with the Parsons woman. She barely admitted that he came to see her, but was very vague as to times he came and left," Karen said defensively.

"I have something else about him," Sarah added, "For the trip to Middlefield area for the past two visits, he rented a car. He rented a 2013 Ford Fusion, black, two weeks ago.

His last visit rental was the day before Amanda's murder; it was a 2013 Chevrolet Equinox, also black."

"What about our other two suspects?" Karen asked.

"Evans, as we probably expected is the least traveled. His wife is very sick and he tends to her. He has made two trips to Atlanta and one to Middlefield. The Middlefield one was on the day of Amanda's murder."

"What? Why didn't you tell us this before?"

"Karen, please, there has been so much going on that this is the first real chance we have had to talk about it," Sarah defended herself.

"Okay, Sarah, I understand. Did he also rent a car?"

"Not that I can tell."

"Have you been able to tell why he was here?"

"From the charges on his card, he paid for gas and he paid for a hotel in town the night before Amanda's death. The Postal Service was holding a retired employees' banquet. That's why he was here. He checked out before noon the next day and bought gas at one p.m. at Robert's Fuel."

"I wonder what he did all day? What kind of car does he drive?"

"He has a black 2015 Chevrolet sedan. I checked with Florida DMV.

"What did witnesses say about the strange car in Amanda's yard before her body was found?"

"It was a black car but no one really noticed so it could have been any black car, SUV or not," Richard answered.

"What about Griswold?"

"I couldn't find any travel records for him."

"Since I interviewed him, I may be able to answer that. I didn't include it in my report specifically, but Frank told me that he doesn't believe in credit cards and prefers to use cash. It didn't seem important at the time, but in view of our feelings about him now, I can see the potential," Susan said.

"All of us are a bit sloppy in our reporting; that includes me. I think we can cut Green some slack in how he did his job," Karen chided.

"So we can't prove whether or not Griswold was in Middlefield on the day of Amanda's murder. Great!" Richard said with a sneer.

"No, we can't Richard," Susan retorted. "But he did tell me that he often comes up this way when he wants to get away."

"Okay, Folks, before we come to blows over this, let me summarize what we've learned today about the day Amanda died: Evans was here on some official business; Griswold may or may not have been here, we can't prove it either way; Williams was here. All have or had black cars by some coincidence on the day of Amanda's murder. Would you say that we have gotten any further with this case?"

"Let's be fair, Karen. We have all been under stress to solve Amanda's murder; it is fraying nerves," said Richard.

"I know that I've been pushing pretty hard. We all need

a break. It's the end of the week. Let's tend to our own family affairs and return on Monday to start again."

"I'm taking Aretha to Atlanta to the Aquarium. She's been there; I haven't," said Richard.

"I loved it there. I couldn't imagine how they got all the whales into those tanks. It is spectacular!" Susan said.

"As usual these days, I'll be alone this weekend, unfortunately. David has to fly to a medical conference in San Francisco. He is not due back to Middlefield until the end of next week when he gets his scheduled break from the Reservation work."

"Join Aretha and me in Atlanta."

"Thanks, but you two love birds need time to yourselves. I'll be okay. Thanks, anyway; I appreciate your asking me. Frankly, something is bugging me about these cases. I think I'll take the quiet weekend to review the facts and reflect on what we are doing. See you all Monday."

Chapter Twenty-One

On Monday morning, Karen opened her eyes to see the bright Georgia sun clearing the tree line facing her home. She missed David, her lover and husband. It was always a joy to wake up beside him and look at his handsome face.

Those mornings she could see faint lines beginning to show around his eyes; sure signs of aging and indications of the stress he faced from the daily responsibilities he carried.

David's medical career at Middlefield General Hospital had blossomed and he was considered one of the best surgeons in the area. His private practice had grown to a point where he had expanded it with partners to meet the needs of his patients.

This morning she dreamily thought of their last night together before he had flown to Arizona to fulfill his sense of giving back to those whose lives did not have the same opportunities he had had. She had supported David to pursue that dream and return to her when it was over. He would be away for nearly a year with only one week at home spaced at the end of each quarter. Regardless of that, wedded life with him had been all that Karen had ever wanted and needed a marriage to be.

Thoughts of her prior life often intruded into the world she now lived and loved. The painful memories that often haunted her were horrible reminders of the ordeal, which had threatened her life and had taken her baby's life. That she had come through the torment with her spirit and sense of worth intact spoke of her inner strength. Though she was unaware of it on this morning, she would need that strength again.

Karen was well aware that her career had reached a plateau. Her daily responsibilities to her team and the City were becoming less attractive. The current murder case coupled with the Forrester cold cases were beginning to occupy more of her private time than she could allow. Her sense of potential failure to solve a current murder and the old, old Forrester cases lay heavily on her mind. She was unsure how she would tell David that she needed to change.

Her effectiveness as a leader of the MCU, she felt, was rapidly waning and the esteem that her team had shown her was beginning to fade. Karen knew that to continue doing this kind of work, she would have to transform the environment around her. She began to dread the thoughts of having to uproot herself and leave for another position elsewhere. It was a thought too upsetting to consider soon, but she knew it would have to be done.

David, of course, could not and would not ever leave his medical world to follow her. She could not be so selfish to even ask him although she felt certain that if she did, he would.

That was the nature of his love for her; she was sure. He had said it many times, but those were moments when things are uttered, but can not be accomplished. David always seemed to have the right advice for her when she needed it. Would it be there now? They would talk when he returned.

Karen was at a career crossroads with no choices that were acceptable. She could not quit in the middle of this investigation. Until David returned, the only option was to plod along and hope for the best. It was this Karen who had to face her team this morning.

* * *

"Good morning, Folks. How was your weekend?" Karen said in as cheerful a voice as she could.

After the small talk subsided, Karen brought the meeting to the point of her concern.

"This weekend I had time to think more about the Amanda Griswold murder. It is my feeling that Amanda had knowledge of who killed the Forresters, but for some reason, which I cannot explain, I believe that she wasn't murdered because of that. She got us involved when she didn't have to. Why would she do that?"

"Could it be that after all this time, the killer figured out that Amanda knew who it was? Her fear of the killer coming after her may have caused her to contact us," Susan replied.

"If we could find that out, we have our killer," Sarah responded.

"Obviously that may be part of the mystery, but we still have no idea of the motive to kill her today." Susan retorted.

"We've guessed she was blackmailing someone; that she killed the Forresters; that she didn't kill the Forresters, but Frank did; where does this circus of speculating stop?" Richard interrupted.

"That's true, Richard, but the fact that Amanda said she found the letters that day of the Forrester murders makes me believe that one of our three suspects felt threatened by her. That to me could be the motive," Susan countered.

"Susan, you have great faith that Amanda told us the truth about the letters, about the issues with Frank and Marisa. Frankly, we really have nothing to go on here," Richard pushed.

"I believe it is one of the three. I don't care what your theory is right now," Susan sputtered.

"Okay, but which one of the three? And why did she wait so many years to 'fess up,' if I might ask?"

"All right you two," Karen chided, "I think we have to take another look at the letters she found. Two of them, as you know, are unreadable, but the third still may give us something. Perhaps we missed something earlier.

"I, for one, am convinced that the letters to Marisa were written by a very troubled woman. I ask you, why would Amanda keep them? If she were the letter writer, I can't believe that she would have contacted us, much less told us about the letters. They are incriminating. Amanda did not write them."

"Are you willing to stake your reputation on that belief?" Richard asked with a sneer.

"Well, we know that the letter was signed with an A and ended with a mouse chewed letter a. Do any of our suspects have names that start with an A and end with an a? The answer is no and no man would write a letter like that anyway," Karen returned.

"Only three women that we have spoken to fit that criteria: Anna Smithson, Amanda Pierce, and Amanda Griswold," Susan said.

"Well, Karen, if it wasn't Amanda Griswold, then it was Anna. Let's arrest her," Richard said with an irritating smugness in his voice.

"Richard, you are becoming exasperating" Karen said. "Try stopping the venom and help. How do you know it wasn't Amanda Pierce who wrote the letters?"

"I don't. From the interviews we did, she and her husband were socially connected with the Forresters. Again, my trusty gut doesn't believe they were involved in any way."

"Gut feeling is not good enough in court, so stop the sophomoric arguments."

"I apologize, Karen, but I don't feel we are making any progress. Should we talk to Anna Smithson again?"

"I do. I think that Susan should ask her come to the station for another talk," Karen said.

"Okay, Karen, I will give her a call. What if she refuses?"

"Tell her she has a choice: talk to us or we will be forced to consider her a suspect in the Forrester and Griswold killings."

"That's not going to help at all, Karen," Richard said.

"It may not, but she may be intimidated enough to think strongly enough about it to cooperate."

"What if she gets a lawyer?"

"We'll cross that bridge when we come to it," Karen answered with a shrug. Let's get back to Amanda's murder. Amanda said there was a fourth letter, which Frank took and hid, but she said that she could not find it. She said that she had not read it."

"Somehow, I really doubt that, Karen," Richard said.

"You are probably correct, Richard; we have no way of knowing," Susan interrupted.

"Well, if she wasn't killed because of the Forresters' murders, then we might assume her murder was random. I am having a tough time accepting that," Richard exclaimed.

"It can't possibly be random, Richard. The pistol used to kill Amanda was the same one used to kill the Forresters. Did you forget that?" Susan countered.

"Also, our three suspects knew Amanda; why would they make the mistake of faking a suicide using the wrong hand?" Sarah asked.

"I agree, Susan, it's too much of a coincidence that some stranger would walk in and kill her using the same pistol used on the Forresters," Sarah responded.

"There is a connection to the Forresters' murders and her killing; we have to find it. It is obvious that something changed after we received Daniel's letter. Once we announced to the world that the Forrester case was being re-opened, people got very nervous," Karen declared.

"Is there any chance that we overlooked something in the Griswold's safe?" Susan asked.

"No, there was a fire-stop at the bottom, so nothing could have slipped down into the wall," Richard replied.

"It can only mean that at some point, Amanda removed the fourth letter or Frank is lying to us," Karen said.

"But why would she have removed the letter?"

"The information about the letters' existence was unknown at the time of Green's investigation, but remember that when we re-opened the case, that bit of information made its way to the public. It's my guess that whoever wrote that letter must have then realized that Amanda had it," Karen answered.

"She either told the wrong person and it got back to the letter writer, or possibly she may have told the writer for blackmail reasons," Richard suggested.

"Look, Richard, we haven't been able to check on Frank's movements to Middlefield prior to Amanda's killing. We have speculated that he may have come here; killed her and then took the letter with him. Maybe he destroyed the letter later," Karen emphasized.

"Was Frank allowed into the house unsupervised, because if he was; he probably has the letter," Sarah cautioned.

"No, we did not allow him to enter the house without us.

We asked him to show us the safe place, which he did. He was not allowed into the house after that. If he didn't kill Amanda and take the letter, we need to find it. Let's get moving," Karen said firmly.

"In my mind, Frank is still an obvious suspect, but we have nothing substantial to tie him to her murder," Richard said not letting go.

"I still don't understand why she got us involved; she certainly didn't need to after all this time," Susan ventured.

"She was scared. She had stirred the pot; she knew someone was after her. It was time to get us involved, for all the good it did."

"Yes, Karen, she was up to her ears in this whole situation with the Forresters. How convenient that she 'found' the letter package beside Stillwater Creek! Did she also find the gun?"

"You have a point, Richard. She played a pivotal role in the investigation of the deaths of the Forresters by hiding the letters and perhaps the gun, but I don't believe that she killed them. However, I believe she knew who did, and that knowledge cost her her life," Karen asserted.

"Without that letter, we are just going around in circles. Everything that we conjecture is just that; our supposing who did what," Susan complained.

"Well, if Frank isn't Amanda's killer and he doesn't have the fourth letter, it must be in that house," Karen suggested.

"And if Frank wasn't the killer, then the real killer may

have taken the incriminating letter. We are wasting our time," Richard nearly yelled.

"I don't mean to throw cold water here, but what do we expect this letter look like, say, or mean?" Susan voiced. "Is it something that we will know when we see it?"

"I understand your concern, Susan, but we have nothing else to try. I want every drawer of every desk pulled out and flipped over. Check the backs of them also. If that doesn't work, I want every piece of furniture examined."

"So you think that he or Amanda hid it in the living room desk? Seems childish to me," Richard retorted.

"Maybe so, but I want a thorough search of any possible hiding place. Get cracking," Karen ordered.

Chapter Twenty-Two

Despite Karen's orders to thoroughly inspect the Griswold house, the indescribable fourth letter was not discovered. Many old notes written by and to Amanda were found in various desk cubbies and page markers in volumes on book shelves, but not a single one having that "something" Karen's crew was seeking.

"Well, I was right, Karen. No letter, no nothing," Richard gloated.

"Yes, you were right, Richard. While you were rummaging in the Griswold house for the past few days, I had a hunch. I asked for a court order to open a safe deposit box in the Middlefield Savings Bank, which was in the name of one Amanda A. Jones. Jones was Amanda's maiden name, which Sarah had discovered from the clerk's office in the town where she and Frank were married."

"I was right. I knew it would be a waste of time at the Griswold's place," Richard retorted.

"I know, Richard, I'm sorry, but it had to be done. Our knowledge of the safe deposit box was also no guarantee; it might have been empty. Amanda had opened the box soon after the Forrester murders. Frank was not on the signature card, so it's doubtful he even knew about it."

"And what did you find?"

"We found a letter. A very important letter, I might add. The fourth letter!!" Karen replied with a smile.

With that exchange, Karen showed them the letter.

Karen watched Richard's and Susan's faces as they absorbed the effect of the writing.

"This is gibberish; how do you know that this is the 'fourth' letter?" Richard asked. "We can't even read it."

Cariad Mae,
Dw i'n dy garu di. Penblwydd Hapus!! Shw Mae? Ni allaf aros gweld chi eto.
Wyr John an y babi?
Rydw i'm dy garu di gymaint. Cym hir byddwn yn gyda'i gilydd. Mae genny gynllun.
Piediwch â rhoi'r gorau!!!
Eich ddilynwr am byth, Tywysog

"Of course I don't absolutely know for sure, but she paid for the box rental all these years. It had to be important to her!"

"Who is going to translate it? I don't even know what language it is," Susan said.

"I've already asked around the station if anyone recognized the language; it is Welsh. Brian Jenkins over in Vice knew what it was. Did you know that Jenkins is a common Welsh surname? Anyway, I gave a copy to him; he said that he would ask his grandfather to translate it for us. We should have it in a few days," Karen answered.

"Didn't you just say that Amanda's maiden name was Jones?" Susan asked.

"I did. I had asked Sarah to do a search of Amanda's background. Her grandparents came to the US in the late forties from Wales. Both Amanda's parents and grandparents have been dead for many years. I believe that someone translated it for her years ago. If that is true, she may have known who wrote it."

Three days later, Officer Jenkins came to Karen's office with a translation. She looked at the original letter and then the translation.

"Things are never easy," she thought. "We achieve one objective and always, another question or hurdle pops up."

"My Grandpa said that he thought it was an intriguing letter. He thought the writer's background may have been Northern Wales, but he can't swear to it. Things are becoming fuzzier to him. He's well over eighty and has been away from Wales for thirty years," Jones shared.

Karen looked at the translation; it's message confirmed her belief that this indeed was the "fourth" letter.

Dear Mae,
I love you. Happy Birthday!! How are you? I can't wait to see you again.
Does John know about the baby?
I love you so much. Soon we will be together. I have a plan.
Don't give up!!!
Your lover forever, Prince

"This may prove our conviction that the Forresters' murders involved a love triangle, which went completely out of control," Karen thought.

"Brian, thank you, thank your grandfather. This is a great help."

"Glad to be useful. Grandpa will be pleased."

"Your Grandpa's idea of Northern Wales may be very important as we close on this case, but at this point I'm not able to tell how much. Again, please thank him for us. His effort is very valuable, Brian," Karen said expressing her gratitude.

"He was happy to do it. It brought back many memories for him."

* * *

Later, Karen met with the MCU.

"Karen, who is Prince?" Richard asked.

"I have no idea; it does confirm our belief that Marisa's behavior had a direct connection with her death. What we can't prove yet is why John was killed."

"Collateral damage, as they say?" Susan responded.

"Interesting method to prevent strange eyes reading it," Richard continued.

"Well, obviously the writer had knowledge of the Welsh language, but that also means that the reader must have been able to read it," Karen said.

"I find it interesting that our three suspects who may have been involved with Marisa Forrester's death knew her as Mae. As we know, Mae was Marisa's nickname to her friends," Susan shared to the group.

"Oh, so Prince was writing to Marisa talking of love and the baby. He clearly thought the baby was his. What was their plan; I wonder?" Richard mused.

"We'll probably never know, but does it exclude him

from the Forresters' murders. He was in love with her," Karen answered.

"We all know that love can turn deadly at a moment's notice," Richard retorted.

"Yes, Richard, how well I know," Karen thought to herself.

"I wonder how Mae was able to read Welsh?" Susan mused. "There is certainly nothing in her background to suggest that possibility."

"I know, Susan, that is what makes this so strange," Karen answered.

"Which of the three men we have interviewed have a Welsh background?" Susan asked.

"All three have surnames whose origins are Great Britain," Sarah asserted.

"Are you kidding me? All three?" Richard said unbelievingly.

"Right, Sarah, you are our resident genealogy expert. Does any one of the three stand out?" Karen asked.

"Not directly, Karen. It's only my opinion, but given what we presently know about the case, my first choice would be Randy Williams, motive and opportunity."

"They all did, Sarah, they were local. How does it tie Williams any closer to the murder than the other two?" Richard pressed.

"Also, Sarah, if he wrote the letter, why would he kill his love? I could see him killing John Forrester, but it doesn't make sense that he would kill Marisa, does it?"

247

Karen pushed.

"Look, Karen, I think Sarah may be onto something. One reason Williams doesn't make sense to me is the interview I had with Anna Smithson, Williams ex. I asked her about Randy's background and she had no knowledge of a Welsh connection, so it wasn't a topic of pillow talk between them," Susan asserted.

"I don't think that proves anything, Susan," Richard responded.

Karen asserted, "Maybe not; I had asked Sarah a few weeks back to get thorough background check on each of them; Green's investigation records don't show any extensive background checks having been done."

"I've been working on them as time permits. It is slow going, and it won't be as complete as we would like," Sarah replied.

"Time is all we have; it would have been handy if Green had done this back in 1979, but, of course, he had no knowledge of the fourth letter; no reason to drag in nationality."

"I found a brief check that Green had done on Williams, but it wasn't what I would call a complete background search," Sarah noted.

"In the meantime, I want us to contact Evans, Williams, and Griswold about this letter."

"Should we phone or visit them?" Susan asked.

"Visit them. Take a copy of the letter. I will see Evans; Susan talk to Griswold, and Richard, it's back to Williams.

You must be forceful and talk about the things we have been discussing. A giveaway to their soul will be the expression on their face when they see it."

Chapter Twenty-Three

Once the visits were complete, the MCU met to discuss their results.

"Well, did Griswold or Williams blanch when you showed them the letter?" Karen asked.

"Williams didn't," Richard replied.

"Griswold didn't either, but he was especially vocal in denying any knowledge of the letter," Susan said.

"It's really suspicious that Frank denies ever seeing that letter. Amanda was adamant in my interview of her that there was a fourth letter at the time she discovered the bundle. She said that Frank saw it and then hid it. If she was telling the truth, the question becomes why did he hide it and deny it now," Karen said.

"For my thinking, it is not strange. Amanda denied ever reading it; I believe that is true. Most likely, at the time, she was not able to translate it; perhaps not recognizing the language it was written in," Richard replied.

"Could it possibly be that the letter Amanda said Frank looked at and then hid was not one of the love letters that Frank said were in the package?" Susan asked.

"Perhaps, but what if Amanda, herself, wrote a letter that day, which she later showed to Frank?" Karen speculated.

"What reason would she have to do that?" Susan probed.

"Given what she knew about the Forresters, perhaps she surmised Frank may have written it and did not want Frank to know of her suspicions," Richard answered.

"If Richard's scenario is realistic; Amanda thought that Frank had killed the Forresters. How could she face living with a killer?" Sarah answered.

"Our theories are becoming surreal; what possible reasons would she have to do that?" Susan said in frustration.

"But assuming that she couldn't read the letter, how would she know the writer's identity?" Sarah pushed.

"Even if Amanda couldn't read the letter, she may have recognized the person's handwriting," Susan responded.

"Who knows; maybe she later showed it to her parents or grandparents to translate; then she squirreled into the safe deposit box," Karen said.

"Sorry my phone's buzzing, I'll be right back," Sarah said.

"Before you go, that is really stretching it, Susan. We are forgetting that Frank's handwriting does not match the letter writer's," Richard said goading her.

"No, Richard, our handwriting expert would only say that certain characters in the letter resembled those of Frank's," Susan responded with a hint of exasperation.

"Then get another expert," Richard demanded.

"Before we do that, Folks, let me go further with this line of conjecture; perhaps Amanda knew it wasn't Frank that wrote the letter, but she may have had some relationship with the writer, which she obviously did not want Frank to know about," Karen continued.

"Karen, how does that line of thinking get us any closer to Amanda's killer?" Richard pressed.

"We feel certain, no, I think we can say that we know that the murder of Amanda was not an opportune, random act by someone who just happened to pick Amanda. The link between her and her killer is the pistol, which we know was also used in the Forrester murders.

"So we can safely assume that her killing ties directly back to the Forrester murders; that is where we have to put our focus now," Karen stressed.

"Sure, Karen, but how and in what way do they connect; obviously none of us can say at this point," Susan emphasized.

"We've previously agreed that a possible motive, is the paternity of Marisa's baby. It is imperative that we prove who was the father of Marisa's baby. The blood typing test done in 1979 only showed that John Forrester could be the father, but it could have been someone else with type B blood; notwithstanding the fact that John had had a vasectomy. Whether it worked or not is anybody's guess at this point," Richard summarized.

"Gordon sent the sample of blood he reserved from the John Forrester post-mortem to the GBI Lab. Sarah sent the swabs from Evans, Griswold, and Williams to the Lab last week. We'll have an answer soon enough provided that John Forrester's sample is still viable. Unfortunately, if one of the other three is found to have been the father, that doesn't prove it was enough of a motive to kill the

Forresters, and it doesn't help us in Amanda's case," Karen added.

"True, Karen, but it does give us a name that we can lean hard on to get a confession, perhaps," Richard declared.

"I think we have to follow the money," Susan offered.

"You mean the money that Amanda was receiving monthly?"

"Yes, Richard, that money," Susan said with an edge in her voice.

At that moment, Sarah re-entered the room.

"Sorry for interrupting, Karen, but I have to tell you that the GBI lab is going to be backed up for several weeks, and that means that our samples won't get tested until they have dealt with their backlog," Sarah said.

"What is causing the delay, Sarah?"

"It's political and worse, it throws a spotlight on the Lab. It's in the newspapers and they're calling the Lab's performance a scandal.

"The Governor has demanded that GBI test some three hundred rape kits that have been sent to them and not tested. Apparently some kits have been at the lab for a few years. The Legislature has threatened to overhaul management if they don't get them done and done accurately. Cases have been languishing waiting for results."

"I understand. Well, we just have to wait. I'll ask Tate to ensure that we are in the queue."

"That puts a stop to our work until we get test results,"

Susan said.

"That's true, but there is nothing we can do about that. We just have to wait," Karen answered. "But in the meantime, Sarah, can you tell us what you found for family backgrounds on the three?"

"I can; it has taken me a number of weeks using several resources to gather the information. There are gaps and some information is sketchy at best.

"I'll list them in alphabetical order. First is Robert Evans; his grandfather, Alun, married a woman named Delyth Eaton in 1915 and they immigrated to the States in 1919 from the port town of Milford Haven in Pembrokeshire, Wales. They had two sons, twins, Morgan, Robert's eventual father, and Hadyn who were born shortly after reaching America. They first settled in New York and then moved to Georgia in 1924 landing in the Middlefield area. Some of what I am saying next; you already know from interviews.

"Hadyn died when he was two. When Morgan was twenty, he married Miriam Smith and they had Robert by 1948. He was their only child.

"Robert went to college and graduated. He married Arlene Carey shortly afterwards. Robert worked as a math teacher for a while. It didn't work out and he took a job at the post office.

"Next in line is Franklin Griswold. His grandparents are native born Americans. His great-grandparents were the immigrants coming from England in the early 1880s. My search didn't reveal any Welsh connections that were evident, but that doesn't mean there are none.

"I could not find any relationships directly to Wales. Griswold may have a Welsh background. It just doesn't show up in the records. There is no reason that he or Evans, for that matter, couldn't have taken an interest in learning Welsh."

"That may be true, Sarah, but very unlikely, wouldn't you say?" Karen said.

"You're probably right, Karen."

"Sure, but that is also true of Randy," Susan said.

"Randy didn't impress me that he had the noodle to learn the Welsh language, much less learn to write it," Richard declared.

"Well, I'm just telling you what I've found out," Sarah bemoaned.

"It's okay, Sarah, please continue."

"Last, we have Randy Williams. His great-grand parents came to America from the town of Tredegar, which is situated on the Sirhowy River in the county borough of Blaenau Gwent, in southeast Wales. They immigrated about the same time as Griswold's folks came from England.

"Their life here seems to be very sketchy, except that his grandfather was in jail in Jacksonville in the forties for theft. So was Randy's father but for vehicular homicide. Randy seemed to rise above it even going to college, but there is no record of his graduating from Florida Central

University or any other college.

"He seems to have not had much ambition; being content to work at menial, handy-man types of work. But again, who is to say that he didn't have the interest in and take the time to learn the language."

"Well, one thing we absolutely know; not one of them admitted any knowledge of the language. Also, there is the puzzle of Marisa's being able to read Welsh."

"You're forgetting, Karen, that we don't even know if Marisa is the Mae of the last letter."

"I stand corrected, Richard, we don't know for certain, but Susan said that Marisa was called Mae by close friends."

"It looks as though we have to wait for the profiles from GBI to move one jot further," Susan said.

"Jot? What's that?" Richard asked with a sneer.

"Come on, you two, give it up. I'm tired of this. Let's break until we get the profiles. We've got other work to complete. I'll call you when I have something. You call me if you become aware anything new related to the case.

"There is one thing that I put in my report of my visit with Robert Evans, but I haven't said to you. His wife, Arlene, is very close to death. Whatever disease she has is progressing very rapidly. He has visiting nurses in to help him daily to take care of her needs. When I was there, he could barely keep his focus to my questions. She probably won't last much longer. He loves her very dearly," Karen explained.

"That's sad, Karen," Susan sympathized.

"Yes, it is. However, I believe that Frank is the enigma in all of this, Folks; his proximity to the Forresters' home; his wife, Amanda's murder; and of course, the damn letters. We talked earlier about following the money. With Frank's 'sugar mama' in the picture, it would be hard to tell if he were the one giving Amanda the extra money each month for the past three years," Karen expanded.

"Let me see what I can find out, Karen," Sarah volunteered.

"Thank you, Sarah. I'll call you all for our next meeting."

After the meeting had broken up, Susan approached Karen.

"How is it going with you personally, Karen?"

"It's okay. I miss David to talk to. Conversations on the phone are not the same. He's due back from Arizona in four weeks."

"I know; Carlos told me that the volunteer work he is doing with indigent children on the Navaho Reservation is outstanding. His surgeon skills are critically needed. He is quite a man!"

"I know, Susan, thank you. He is my life. When he is out of town, I am not able to functions as well as I should. Sometimes I wonder if I shouldn't give this job up."

"What would you do?"

"I haven't told anyone, not even David, but I've been offered a position in the Atlanta FBI office. I was surprised because they usually want lawyer trained folks. The Section Chief said that my skills with codes and ciphers was becoming more critical these days as the threat of terrorism increases."

"Will you take it?"

"It will all depend on what David thinks. I would like a different environment, but…"

"I would miss you very much, Karen. We have been through many rough times, but I can appreciate what you are saying. I have thought the same things myself."

"Well, I'm not going to say anything to David until I can wrap him in my arms."

"That's a smart move. No one likes problems delivered over the phone."

"Yes, even though we use Facetime it isn't the same as being able to touch the person. We do talk every night. He is flying home this weekend; since he's been on this volunteer work, every time he comes back it's like another honeymoon."

"Sounds delicious. Good luck, Karen."

Chapter Twenty-Four

The cell phone rang several times before it was answered.

"David, what time are you arriving in Atlanta tomorrow?"

"Love, I have to cancel this weekend. I have a child who needs immediate surgery. I can't make her wait until I get back. It is life-threatening."

"Oh, I understand, David, but I miss you. It is tough without you to talk to. You always have such good advice. This latest case is driving us around in circles. Your counsel would be just what I need."

"Well, we have time now. What's the matter, Sweetheart?"

"As I told you sometime ago, we have three men who we believe may have been involved with the murder of a couple in 1979."

"Yes, I remember that. What about it?"

"We have their swabs at GBI for profiling. We are trying to find out if one of them fathered the woman's baby. I am not confident that the old blood samples of the baby and the couple taken back then are good enough for comparison.

"What if we accuse the wrong person, or worse, what if none of the three were involved and the baby was actually the husband's?"

"Nothing is a hundred percent, Karen. You know that; if

the samples were preserved well enough, there should be a reasonable chance the tests will work and a comparison would be valid."

"I hope that you are correct. The solution of the current murder of the wife of one of the three may hinge on the profile results. Without them, we cannot construct a reasonable motive for her murder. We speculate that she may have been blackmailing the couple's murderer."

"Who are you talking about, Karen?"

"Amanda Griswold. She was a neighbor of the murdered couple. We found a letter that she kept all these years in a safe deposit box. We suspect this was the reason why she could extort money from the killer. However, that letter doesn't help us identify the killer because it was signed with a pet name for the writer."

"I understand, Sweet, but that is beyond the question you asked me. I feel that the viability of blood samples taken many years ago, if stored properly, provide accurate profiling. There is not much else I can add to that. It really is a 'take it or leave it' situation."

"What you are saying is reasonable. I don't know enough details about the process. The GBI has a mess on their hands so it will take a few more weeks until we get results. I'll take your advice and let the experts do their work. Thank you, Love."

* * *

"Karen, we've finally gotten the profiles of the samples for Evans, Griswold, and Williams. GBI is doing a comparison to Marisa's baby's profile, but they say it will take another couple of days. The rape-kit workload is horrendous; they did the best time-wise for us that they could."

"Thank you, Sarah, I'll give Marcus a call and give him our thanks."

Susan came to Karen's office at that moment, "Front Desk just called to say Robert Evans has notified us that his wife, Arlene has passed."

"That's very sad; I knew it wouldn't be long. She was in bad shape when I was there, but I told you all that already. I will call Robert Evans in a few days to tell him I need to speak with him again."

"Why is that?" Susan asked.

"He said something that has been disturbing me since I last interviewed him. It was about Arlene. He said that he hadn't realized her depth of devotion. I didn't ask him what he meant. I accepted it as a comment on the love of a wife."

"That's unlike you, Karen. You never let things like that slip."

"I have lots of things on my mind these days. I miss David and worry about him all the time. He told me he isn't feeling well these days. He thinks that he is simply overworked, but I am nervous that it's something else. I would like to ask him to come home and terminate the volunteer work. I know that's selfish, but I want him with me."

"That is understandable. You two have only been

married a couple of years."

"It's more than that, Susan; I'm not sleeping well at night. What I spoke to you about the other day is also a worry. I really want to move on; but I'm afraid of the effect on David's and my life if I do. I'm sorry, Susan, I shouldn't trouble you with my private problems. Let's get back to your Smithson interview."

"Okay. I asked Anna again about Randy's behavior with women. Anna said that Randy had an eye for women, but she said she honestly felt that he had not done anything with Marisa."

"Yes, but didn't she say that he told her that something happened that 'should not have happened?' That's why he was fired. The question is why she lied to you about the sometime, onetime affair with Marisa. Randy told us that he did tell her. That's why they ran into marital troubles," Karen replied.

"Yeah, Karen, that's the way her story goes, but really, who knows after all this time? They are both liars in my book. It may have given her the motive for Amanda's murder, if she was blackmailing her, though."

"And we still haven't been able to nail any connection to her or Randy that ties directly to Amanda's murder. So we have nothing on them at this point.

"We know the pistol links the three murders together. Whoever used that gun on the Forresters also used it on Amanda. But who is it? Where has it been all this time?" Karen asked with frustration.

"Cheer up, Karen, when we have the comparison profiles to Marisa's baby, we will have our killer, I believe. Carlos did put my mind at ease about the profile issue."

"David confirmed what Marcus said. What the test results give us are the facts; we should trust to them."

"Yeah, when are they going to get the comparisons back to us?"

"Sarah said Marcus promised by tomorrow. I will let you know when the results arrive."

*   *   *

"Good morning. Marcus called me late last night about the paternity profile comparisons. The actual reports will be here later today, but I can tell you right now that they are disappointing. There is no match to Evans, Griswold, or Williams."

"Karen, they have got to be kidding," Richard nearly shouted.

"No, they are not playing a game; no match. Marcus said that when he realized this, he asked for John Forresters' profile to be compared. The sample James Gordon had preserved was viable. It is a match. He was the father."

"I thought Marcus said earlier that John Forrester was not the father," Susan cried out.

"He did, but there may have been a mix-up on the lab technician's part. The lab manager and the tech have been reprimanded. Marcus says there is no doubt that John Forrester was the father," Karen explained.

"That puts us back to square one; we now have nothing

to tie these three to the Forresters or Amanda, for that matter. Worse, if we ever are able to somehow determine who the killer was, the court case will become a zoo once a defense lawyer knows about the lab mix-up," Richard said dejectedly.

"It does, Richard; I'm very concerned that we have nothing going forward from this point. My bigger fear is that Amanda's case will go cold, also. I'm going to Chief Tate and tell him we have to stop working the Forrester case. Any potential lead we have developed has led us nowhere. I will recommend to him that either you, Susan, or you, Richard remain on the Griswold murder case."

"I'll take it, Karen," Richard volunteered.

"Thank you, Richard. The Chief and the Mayor will not be happy about this decision. We have all given the Forrester kids false hope that we would find their parents' killer."

"No, Karen, they won't just be unhappy; they will be livid and it will be hell around here," Susan said.

"I know, but there is no other choice, which I can see," Karen answered.

"Before you see Tate, Karen, give me one week to try a re-visit to each of our suspects," Richard pleaded.

"Richard, you will be wasting your time. We've been through all of this before," Susan warned.

"I know, but I have a feeling that we have overlooked something. It is just a gut sense; I want to try it to find it."

"Okay, Richard, it will probably not change anything."

Chapter Twenty-Five

The man sat at his favorite desk and began to write in a newly purchased diary. The ancient oak desk with its green felt blotting surface had been with him for over fifty years; it had accompanied him everywhere from his freshman days at college.

The man had been writing his thoughts and fears in a diary for many years, but he always called it his day book. This prose would be different, though; it would stand alone as an admission to his children, and finally the world. He needed them to understand; needed them to forgive and not judge.

At this age, his hands trembled slightly causing perceptible jaggedness in the lines forming the words of his handwriting. No one today would be able to recognize these squiggles from the flowing, beautiful penmanship, which came from this hand in his earlier years.

He and his doctor were aware of the onset of Parkinson's disease, which continued its relentless progress slowly taking over his life. Doctors had warned him that they were not able medically to delay the increasing symptoms affecting his ability to manage his daily tasks.

On this day, as always, the desk and his familiar chair gave him comfort; a sense of peace that had been elusive since that day. His body was failing, but his sharp mind maintained clear-cut images of that horrible time so long ago. Regardless of all his efforts to block the terrible scenes, they had tortured him without end.

The day and time had come to put the entire matter to rest; his family was grown; his wife was close to death; this could not be put off any longer.

He knew things about the fateful day, which no other person knew. The overwhelming sense of guilt and the secrets he had held for over thirty-four years could not be cleansed away until he had set things straight. This way was the only one left to him. Slowly, he began to write…

January 28th

Today Doctor Tom Corridan, my longtime friend, came to tend to Alicia. He told me that there is nothing else to be done for her. We have been expecting this for a long time; the disease is unrelenting; but one is never prepared, though, for that final moment. Tom told me it will be over in a few days. I have to accept that my love will no longer be with me. It has been over thirty-four years since that terrible time; we have been haunted by it ever since.

January 31th

This morning I made breakfast as usual for my dearest. When I came to her bedroom, she motioned me to her side. She whispered something that I didn't understand, and then she was silent. I realized her end was very near. My grief and guilt were overwhelming.

I called Tom. He came to the house around eleven-thirty today to say farewell to my beloved Alicia. And then she slipped into that void we must all enter. I was pleased that Tom was there to support me in my grief.

I broke down with such dreadful pain and sorrow; I cannot bear to think what life will be without her. The loss of my Dearest Alicia and the constant memory of that fateful day so many years ago has driven me to thoughts of my own death.

February 1st

I must pull myself up to support my children; they are flying in for their Mother's funeral. Both are very upset that they were not able to be here to say goodbye.

I will be strong for them. It will take all of my strength; Alicia was my life; I do not know what I shall do with the rest of mine.

I will not write again until I am able to be alone again with my thoughts. I hope I can make the dreadful day to pass without embarrassing myself.

February 4th

The funeral was beautiful if a funeral can be described that way. I miss Alicia in ways that I could never have imagined when she was alive. I protected and provided for her all of our married life; she did the same for me and more. I have lost a huge part of myself; I don't know what I shall do next.

February 5th

My agony at the loss of Alicia is unbearable. I must put an end to it; I cannot go on this way. I lie in bed and have nightmares of the evil I have done with my life. I am terrified of what awaits me when I leave this life; yet, I must reveal all that I can before that day. I must set the record straight. My lies and deceit have made me rue the day I was born.

February 6th

I have kept records for nearly all of my adult life. I have recorded marriages, births, deaths, trials and tribulations of family and friends; volumes of which form an impressive library.

The time has come for me to make my last entries. I have remained silent for too long about that horrible day in July. I must tell this in a way that my family and the police, yes, the police must understand that I am not a fiend.

How I acted that horrible day has haunted me since. The time has come for me to tell the truth. Of course, it will be a shock to my wonderful children, but I hope that they can forgive me. I hope that this *will bring some solace to the Forrester children who have paid a terrible price for simply being born.*

Tom has suggested that I get my affairs in order. He says that he understands the agony I am going through, but he doesn't know the deep and vile reasons for my grief. I have lied to my best friend over the years not having the courage to say what I have kept from the world.

"Affairs in order." What a strange way of saying things. But affairs in order seems right in view of what I have done.

Guilt and Alicia's release have driven the reasons I need to assuage my conscience of the awful facts and tell the story I've so long kept secret. My strength weakens day by day; even if there were things to help me, I would not accept them.

Anyway, I am too old for any heroics to extend my distress filled life. Life had been good until things went so horribly wrong that day so many years ago. It is the sentimentality of an old man who feels he must leave a short biography of his life, but I hope it can help to explain why I acted the way I did back then. I had to defend my actions in many ways to remain sane, but I ruined many lives and that thought haunts me daily.

I cannot beg for forgiveness; I do not deserve it; I only wish to be understood. I am tired tonight. I will write again tomorrow.

February 7th

I will start this account with my parents, for without them, there would be no story for me to relate. My mother and father were born at a time when the world was very different from today.

My parents' upbringing had all the advantages of the social and financial luxuries of their generation, which allowed them to attend colleges their parents considered to be some of the best. And so, they were trundled off to college at the tender ages of eighteen.

My father earned his degree in American History and my mother earned hers in English Literature. The fact that they met at all was truly a chance situation. The two colleges were close to each other geographically being only ten miles or so distant. As luck would have it, they met at a social function arranged by his fraternity, and as they told the story, it was love at first sight.

After graduation, they wed in what was known in the local papers as the wedding of the decade. They settled in a rural Connecticut town where both taught high school for several years, after which, they decided to move to the town of Sylvania, Georgia to avoid the snow and cold of the winters.

It was in Sylvania that my brothers and I were born and lived throughout our early years. My birth was the last of the three children (all boys) that my mother had borne in her marriage to my father.

I was born on Friday the thirteenth in January of 1945. My mother told me that some people thought I was bad luck baby being born on the 13th. I didn't believe in such superstitions, but in view of what happened in my life; maybe they were right.

Our parents' philosophies and habits of life required that nothing be left to chance. Thus my brothers and I were each fifteen months apart in age proving that the two had studiously planned out the conception and births of their children.

February 8th

Over the years, I had learned that my maternal grandparents had come from oil money and my paternal grandparents from the benefits of Prohibition bootlegging.

Whatever the reason for the family wealth, most was spent or wasted and very little made it into the pockets of my parents after my grandparents' deaths.

My brothers and I never met either set of grandparents as all had died from various ailments and accidents relatively soon after our parents had completed their degrees and settled down south. If well-connected and wealthy aunts and uncles were in the family, we had never been informed of their existence.

For all their planning and philosophy of rearing a

family, our parents did play favorites with me and my brothers.

Until her dying day she protected and loved her three children, but it was for me that she saved her special feelings.

She always defended me when spats arose between me and my brothers. I would gloat, but they seemed to bear me no grudge as our mother's darling. Now when I look back on it, it shaped my early years; perhaps not for the better.

My two brothers were always "sports this and sports that," which pleased Dad. I was always the bookworm attaining high grades while my brothers just seemed to scrape by, which annoyed my mother while my father paid my achievements little notice; praising my brothers for their prowess on the fields.

February 9th

At age eighteen, I received acceptance to college leaving the comfort of friends and family to study and learn the ways of the world. I decided to focus my education on the math world, and I placed on the Dean's List every semester. Graduation led to Graduate School where after two years, I obtained my Master's Degree.

My two brothers did not attend college; married young, and moved to far off places. Both died within four years of each other leaving no children. My line was to be the one to carry on the name.

When it was time to come back to the home area, I took up a teaching position offered at the local high school. In due time, I re-met and married a woman, whom I had known from my school days.

Our life together went well for a few years until I found that I could not support a family on my teacher's pay. Alicia and I had agreed that if we had children, one of us would not work and the other would have to find a better paying line of work. Being the man, I left teaching and found a much better paying job.

In due course, we had two children; both are now grown with families of their own; they hold responsible career positions. My son now lives in California and my daughter lives in Missouri. I am proud of them.

We were a happy family; life was what Alicia and I wanted, but just when things were going well, I spoiled the life Alicia and I had worked so hard to achieve.

I remember well when this nightmare started. It had begun innocently enough as situations often do. Alicia and Marisa Delgado had become friends, rather, acquaintances a few years after her marriage to John Forrester. I was their mailman; it was I who introduced them.

One day, Marisa told Alicia that her marriage was

spiraling downward; she could not take John's abuse any longer in her marriage; she was planning to get a divorce. Marisa had nursing ambitions; which John did not appreciate nor would he allow her to pursue. Marisa's options were few and she knew leaving John was dangerous, but she felt she had to get away.

What Alicia did not know was that a year before, Marisa had asked me if I would be willing to tutor her in math since she wanted to be prepared when she would start work on another degree, and math was her weak subject. Since I had mathematics degrees, Marisa thought that I might be of help to her. I was reluctant to tutor Marisa; it would take time away from my family; lessons would have to be prepared and corrected. I told her I couldn't help.

After Marisa's admission about her marriage, Alicia was sympathetic and strongly urged me to help our friend. I warned Alicia that it was not a good idea, but she prevailed; I told Marisa that I would tutor her.

February 10th
My true reasons for not becoming involved was my attraction to Marisa. I should have recognized my weakness; told Alicia about it and pulled away from the agreement. But I didn't.

Meeting logistics became the first order of

concern. It would have been nearly impossible to come to our house because of Mae's two young children. I suggested to Mae that we meet for lessons at her house; she suggested it might be best when her husband was at his club meetings, since we all knew that John was very jealous.

Marisa proposed Tuesdays at seven would work for the meeting times, since John met with friends in Atlanta that day. His usual routine was that John often did not return until midnight.

And so our tutoring meetings began. Mae always ensured that the two children, Daniel and Patsy were in bed before I arrived to prevent Daniel from saying anything to John about my visits.

I found that Mae was a good student completing all the weekly assignments by the time we would next met. Sessions usually took about an hour and we would go over each problem and I would show her what mistakes she had and how to approach similar problems. Then I would give her the next assignment and leave for home.

One evening, after the math session had been completed, Mae offered me a glass of wine. My first reaction was to refuse, but then I thought better of it. We sat down to talk about things of no special import. Finishing my drink, I left for home, but I knew that something had changed.

I decided not to say anything to Alicia about it;

she trusted me and I was deeply in love with her. I knew then things might be getting out of my control; thoughts of being alone with Mae excited me; I knew where this would lead, but I felt compelled to continue seeing her.

I did fear John. If he found out that I was spending any time alone with Mae, he would probably kill the both of us. John would not believe that the math lessons were innocent. In time, his distrust would be validated.

I had a family and wanted nothing to disrupt that; yet, I was drawn to Mae, making me feel helpless. I knew that I should stop the sessions; I realized that I was weak. I rationalized that I was trying to help another person and that was innocent enough.

I was a coward and felt I should tell my wife about it. No, she would not understand and the friendship between the two friends would end. No, I felt it was better left unsaid. It was unwise and deceitful of me. It did not stop.

After that first wine session, when lessons were done, Mae always offered wine and I always accepted. We would drink more wine than we should; soon we began having more intimate conversations, which had nothing to do with theorems and proofs.

One evening, conversation and actions led to something that should not have happened; we *became intimate as I had known and wanted to happen. We were both remorseful, but not enough to stop; it happened every lesson after that evening. I felt guilty for cheating on my wife, but I could not and would not stop.*

I tried to rationalize my behavior with Mae. Couldn't a person love two people intensely at the same time? Was that so wrong? Why couldn't love unite two people in separate relationships without one or the other being hurt?

I knew that this reasoning was just to assuage my own guilty conscience. I did not know then what would happen to change all of our lives in a horrible way.

It was during this time that we began to write letters to each other, love letters, which later come to haunt us. We both had sworn to destroy the letters, but...

Chapter Twenty-Six

Karen sat in her office trying to find the words she would use to announce the state, or rather failure, of the MCU's investigation into Amanda's murder. She had given Richard additional time with little enthusiasm on her part to re-contact the three suspects to try to close the case.

After that, if no new clues or evidence surfaced, she would have to tell Chief Tate that Amanda's murder would not be solved by them, or perhaps, ever. That news would rattle the Mayor and the Chief; possibly enough to end her career in law enforcement. In a few more days, she would have to stop postponing the inevitable report to Tate.

To distract her from the enormity of her and the Team's failure to find a solution to the three murders, Karen turned her thoughts to the personal side of her life.

She thought of David's imminent return from the 'four corners' area of Arizona. His four-month tour medically ministering to the Navaho Nation was finally done and even though he had periodically flown home during that time to spend mini-honeymoons with Karen, this time she hoped he would be home for good. Thoughts which had no place in her office had been cluttering her thought process all morning. Tonight was the night!

A call from Chief Carter of the Orlando Police shattered the silence of Karen's office. The ringing of her phone brought her out of her reverie and she answered, "Karen Hunter, here. Who is calling, please."

"This is Chief Daniel Carter from Orlando, Florida. At you Chief's request, we sent a technician out to Robert Evans' home two weeks ago to obtain a DNA sample."

"Yes, thank you. We have already received the profile results, which for us were disappointing. Thank you again for your support."

"You are welcome, Major Hunter. The reason for this call is to inform you that we received a 911 call this morning from Robert Evans' home. This is premature, but the coroner has made a preliminary judgement that Mr. Evans has committed suicide."

"Chief, that is terrible news. I had interviewed him several weeks ago. One of my detectives was scheduled to interview him again on a matter we have; he called me yesterday to report that he was going to Evan's home tomorrow..."

"I don't mean to interrupt you, but his wife, Arlene recently passed away."

"I knew that his wife was very ill and not expected to live too much longer. In fact, he had let us know of his wife's passing."

"We notified his son and daughter of their father's death. They said that their mother and father had been extremely close and were deeply in love even after many years of marriage. They said that they were concerned when they were here for their mother's funeral that their father might be suicidal. They told him of their concerns, but he said that that was nonsense. It looks as though they may have been correct.

"In the course of going through Evans' home, we came upon a journal, a day book, really, on his desk. Reading the latest entry, which was rather long, I called your Chief. We both feel that it should be turned over to you because it relates to a case that you have been working. The journal entry makes statements, which appear to explain a murder case that occurred many years ago. I will send it along to you."

"Thank you, Chief Carter. This case has been frustrating from the very first day we started. I hope that this journal sheds some light."

"I hope it helps; I will get it to you as soon as possible."

"Thank you again, Chief; I look forward to it. I can have my Detective pick it up, if you agree. One more thing; were there any more journals in the house?"

"As a matter of fact, there are. It appears that he kept his day books for many years."

"Would you check to see if journals for 1978 through 1981 exist?"

"He has quite a library. I will have my men check for those dates. If they are there, I will give them to your detective once the Medical Examiner has made his firm determination regarding the death of Mr. Evans."

"Thank you, Chief. We owe you."

* * *

Three days later, Richard arrived at the Middlefield PD late in the afternoon with the journals. Karen assembled the

MCU to assess what had been delivered to them.

"Since it is late in the day, I suggest that we meet tomorrow to start reading the journals with fresh minds. I am as eager as you to see what Evans has to say, but, frankly, this case has been so frustrating, I can wait one more evening to be disappointed again," Karen said with some dejection.

"Can I take one of the journals to read tonight?" Richard asked.

"No, this is a team effort and we should all work together on them. Let's meet at eight tomorrow morning and see what he has to say. Good night, see you all in the morning," Karen answered.

* * *

The next day, the team began to read through the journals starting with the oldest. Each took a few journals to peruse.

"So far, this is a pleasant life story that Evans is painting, but I am beginning to think we will learn nothing beyond what we don't already know," Richard said.

"We have to be patient. The man was in pain; perhaps he will…"

"I've had enough of lies and other ways these people have dreamed up to misguide us," Richard voiced interrupting Susan.

"You know, Richard, sometimes you get on my nerves with your irritating, know it all attitude," Susan retorted in frustration.

"Well, sometimes it is very tough to work with two women who always seem to hold information between them," Richard rejoined.

"Enough whining, Folks. We have enough problems with this case without you going at each other's throats. I know that this is wearing on all of us, but we have to pull together to finish this. These journals are the best news we've had. Let's continue," Karen ordered.

"Okay, Karen, but would it make more sense to start with the latest one?" Richard pushed.

"Why do you suggest that?"

"Because it is the one written just before his death."

"Okay, my nerves can't take this much longer. Richard, you read it to us just like we were in the first grade," Karen said.

"I will be happy to do that," Richard responded.

Chapter Twenty-Seven

A couple of months later Mae told me at one of our sessions that she was pregnant. I was elated for her; it was then that she told me the child was mine. I couldn't believe my ears; she had told me that she was on birth control. I was indignant at first.

How did she know it was my child? Her reply devastated me; she knew for certain because John had recently had a vasectomy and I was her only lover. John couldn't be the father. I told her that vasectomies don't always work; she said that John's did, end of issue.

I panicked and went home wondering how I would get myself out of this mess. I did not have the courage to tell Alicia that I had fallen in love with Mae and worse, that she was carrying my child. Still, I loved Alicia with all my heart. How could I say that to her?

It took me several days to build up courage to confess that Marisa and I had been intimate. I did not tell Alicia that Marisa was pregnant.

When I did admit what had happened, Alicia reacted in a way I didn't understand. She told me that she loved me and that she would not live without me. My mistake would not end her love for me. She said that she would never leave me. She had married me for better or worse, and would not leave me or the children. I could not believe it!

I asked how we could possibly stay friendly with Marisa. Her reply was that hatred never solved anything; it was important not to destroy her family or ours.

Alicia's love came with a condition though, she warned me to stop the relationship; I promised that I would; it was another lie; I continued my infatuation with Mae. Even through all this trouble, Mae and I could not leave each other alone. It was sordid, but we were weak and could not stop. I knew that Alicia would not forgive me now.

Later Mae told me that someone was writing her threatening letters. She was frightened, but obviously could not tell John about them. I asked her if she had any idea who had written them. She said that she had no inkling of who it could be.

Several neighbor's wives had let her know that they thought she was coming on to their husbands, which Mae denied. I believed her. Who could be the writer puzzled us both.

Much later, to add to my shame, I asked Mae if she would get an abortion. My callousness showed itself; I wanted to play but not pay. I knew that once it became known to the world about her condition, my life with Alicia would be over.

No, was her answer. I asked how would she handle this with John? She said that she had no choice but would have to tell him. I said that he would probably kill us both.

She said that if he did forgive her, she would stay with him. She would never leave her children and John would never let her take them with her. I had destroyed two families.

February 12th
The thought of that deadly July afternoon comes back to me every day. I was on my rounds; I had a package to deliver to John. As I went to the porch, I heard voices that were garbled. I suspected that John had come home for lunch and they had gotten into a fight.

I had a pistol, which I always carried. Fearing that John would hurt her, I went crashing through the front doorway, I saw the horror in the living room. Mae lay on the sofa with stab wounds, blood everywhere.

John was covered with blood and he was crying. He held a knife in his hand; I yelled for him to drop it. I told him to sit down; the room began to spin. He had killed my Mae and my baby.

I told him that I was going to kill him. John began begging for his life. I raised the pistol close to his head and fired. My hatred spilled out and I sent another bullet into his chest. My rage was uncontrollable.

I went to Mae; cried as I said I love you. She struggled to breathe. The gurgling sounds coming from her were horrible; my love was dying before my eyes. I had destroyed a person I loved. What I had done to John would destroy me also.

As she struggled to take breaths, Mae tried to say something. I placed my ear near her lips. "Why did this…" she struggled to ask, then. "Help me," she whispered through torturous moaning. "Help me."

I could not help her, and I could not let her suffer. I raised the pistol to her temple and fired. The moaning and breathing stopped. I had killed Marisa and our baby. John was slumped on the couch; I had killed him in a fit of rage. The horror of what I had done overwhelmed me. I went into the kitchen to rinse some of the blood that had splattered on me. I went back into the living room to see if I had left any trace of myself. Even then I was thinking about getting away as I walked to the front door.

Tears would not stop coming as I started to leave the hideous sight behind, but the two children came out of their bedroom crying. They ran to their parents trying to hug them; tracking through the blood. I went to them and picked them up. Now we were all bloody. I took them to the porch and saw Amanda Griswold looking at me from Stillwater Bridge. I called for her to call 911; Marisa had been murdered. As I held the children, time seemed to have stopped, but ten minutes later, the police arrived.

The police took the children from me; they were sobbing and did not want to leave me; the intense questioning began. No one had thought to check me for any weapon; a week later I placed it into a safe deposit box where it sat for over thirty years. I loathed that pistol and never wanted to see it again.

The detective grilled me for several hours. He finally let me go home to clean up. I had answered all their questions.

My heart was pounding and I didn't know how I would explain what had happened at the Forresters to Alicia. I could not believe that John had stabbed her. Was he so enraged that he needed to erase her and the child?

As I drove home, selfish thoughts crowded my mind. Could I ever tell Alicia that I had killed Mae? How could I tell her about shooting John? She had forgiven me for being unfaithful, but she would never forgive me for murder and I knew it. She would call the police and I would go on death row until...

When I got home, Alicia was very calm and began asking me what had happened at the Forresters'. I was so surprised at her question that I stuttered and stammered until she said that she already knew that Marisa and John were dead.

She said that Amanda Griswold had called to tell

*her that someone had killed the Forresters. She told
Alicia that I had discovered the bodies.*

*It puzzled me that Amanda Griswold would say
that both Forresters had been killed. I rationalized
that Amanda had been interviewed by the police, but
they would not have let her into the crime scene.*

*Alicia said that Amanda had told her that Marisa
had been horribly stabbed by John and then he was
shot, but who had done that was a mystery. Why
would the police have told Amanda that? Usually,
police try to hold crime details from the public.
Details often trip up suspects.*

*In my grief and guilt, I wanted to shower right
away and calm myself down, but Alicia was insistent
for my side of the story. I could not tell her that when
I had hugged Mae for the last time, her blood had
gotten onto my shirt. My act of picking up Patsy and
Daniel in their bloody clothes had fooled the
detectives. They assumed that was how I got blood
all over my clothes. Blood was drying into a sticky
mass on my uniform where blood splatter from my
two victims had drenched me.*

*She asked for such detail that the guilt of what I
had done finally made me realize what I had done. I
told her about coming upon the conditions in Mae's
home and the pathetic crying of their two frightened
children.*

I could not confess my role to her. I told her that I

thought John had stabbed Marisa; then shot her and himself. I hoped she would never know that John had been shot twice. Such was my deception.

I could not control my crying. Alicia hugged me trying to comfort me, but my pain was overwhelming. We agreed that we would not talk again about the Forresters' deaths. They had been friends, but now they were gone.

Our life together was too precious to tear apart. I was stunned at what she said. Did she know that I had a part in the murders? Was it her intuition or had Amanda Griswold guessed the truth and said something? If Alicia believed that I killed the Forresters, she did not ever say it to me.

Nevertheless, I cannot say how relieved I was that the love of my life would stand by me, but the guilt of what I had caused and done has never left me. I had loved two women equally and had murdered one and also her husband. There was a place in Hell for me. I could never purge my conscience nor atone for my murderous rage.

The horror of what John had done and what I had had to do plagued me every day. Nightmares occurred every time I tried to sleep. Alicia had to waken me many times to stop my screaming when John, covered in blood, would point to me and shout in a grating voice, "Killer, killer." I tried to put this filthy apparition out of my mind, but it appeared many nights.

Then, one year to the day of the murders, Alicia and I were sitting at the kitchen table. I had had a terrible night's sleep. Suddenly Mae and John were standing before us. John had appeared in my nightmares many times, but never Mae and never during daylight. I was stunned; my hands began to tremble.

"What do you want from me?" I heard myself ask.

"You were deceived by circumstance and love. We forgive you," they said in unison; then disappeared.

I turned to my wife, but it seemed to me that she had not seen them. She asked what I meant by my question. I lied and said it was nothing.

I did not understand what they had said about circumstance and love. How could they forgive me? It made no sense. It was only my imagination; how could it make sense?

After that day, my nightmares became less frightening, but daily I was torn about confessing to the police, but I couldn't. I rationalized why. I was right to stay silent; I had my wife and children to care for. I pretended that I was innocent of taking Mae's and John's lives.

I knew that John had stabbed Mae; I had rendered justice. It was a sick idea, but I had no other way to keep my sanity, but I had killed Mae; perhaps she would have lived!

Was I wrong about John? They had forgiven me for my crimes. Why? That question haunted me.

As the years went by, and no one was ever charged with the murders, I began to relax believing that I would never be caught.

Three years ago, Amanda called me and said that she had found some love letters on the day of the murders. She said she thought that they might interest me. Amanda told me that she had not given the letters to the police; that she and Frank had read them. She said that she knew who killed the Forresters, but Frank did not.

She said that she had wanted to tell the police exactly what she had seen and heard on the day of the murders, but they didn't want to get involved. I asked what that was.

She said that she had seen a car leaving Mae's home just before I drove up. John had arrived at the house at his usual time for lunch just after the car left and only had been there a few minutes before I arrived.

She told me that she saw me stop at the house. Shortly after I went into the house, she had heard gun shots. She kept watching the house.

It was only after I had carried the children to the porch that I had noticed her walking with her dog and yelled for her to call 911. I suspected then that she knew what I had done. I asked her why she waited all these years to contact me. She said that I was her rainy day fund.

I asked her what she wanted to keep quiet. She answered that if I could pay her some money each month, she could forget what she saw. She said things could go on as usual.

I gave her what I could from my meager retirement pay. She has been bleeding me for money each month ever since to keep her quiet.

Sometime ago, a Middlefield police detective began asking many questions, forcing me to re-live that terrible day. The detective said they had re-opened the investigation into the Forresters' murders. I was scared and may have said stupid things to her, but I hoped that I didn't say anything suspicious to the detective.

After that visit, my nightmares and dread began again. My hands trembled and I was distracted so that my thoughts were confused. It is very difficult to write this, but I must free my conscience.

Shortly after the detective visited me, I received a call from Amanda. She gave me more information about the letters. She said that Mae had given them to her for safekeeping a week before her murder. She had told Amanda that she feared something bad was going to happen, and she did not want anyone to know about them.

Amanda said that she had found many letters in

the packet. She knew that all the love letters had been written by me, but she didn't share that information with Frank. There were three hateful letters also. The love letters and the three threatening ones were the letters that she showed to Frank. There was a special fourth one her husband knew nothing about.

After they both had read the love letters, they decided to store them where fortunately for me, most had been chewed by mice. The special fourth letter was in pristine condition since she had hidden it in a separate place.

She said that re-opening the case had scared her and she wanted to give them to the police. She told me that she had called the police and that they had come to her house to collect those three chewed up letters, but not the fourth. She wondered if I would like to buy the fourth letter. I asked her what she wanted for the letter.

She said that she wanted ten thousand dollars, and if I couldn't come up with the money, she would tell the police what she knew including the fourth letter.

I told her I would come up with the money somehow; eventually, we agreed on a date for us to meet at her house. I knew that I could not come up with ten thousand dollars, but I had no choice. I lied, I had to get my hands on the letter.

On that day, I went to her home. We talked for a few minutes while she pretended to retrieve the letter *from the desk. As I gave her the fake package of money, she did not check it. The witch mentioned again about the car that she had seen leaving that day just before I had arrived.*

I asked her for more details about the car. She said she had walked nearly to Mae's house when she saw a young women running to a white Chevrolet. She said that the woman had blood on her dress. She knew who it was.

Then she said something stupid; she said that she felt that she needed to tell the police after all these years. They were coming to interview her again in a few days.

She was not going to ruin my life at this point. As Amanda prattled on, I reached into my pocket; pulled out my pistol and aimed it at her. She started to scream; I pushed her into a chair and fired a shot directly into her head. I wiped the gun clean and put it into her hand. I then wrapped her hand around the pistol grip and pulled the trigger with her finger. It would look like a suicide, I hoped. I scooped up the 'money' package and searched for the letter. I could not find it. I panicked.

I knew I had to get out of there fast, but leaving the letter was agony. Then I thought that Amanda had scammed me. The letter did not exist. Mae had assured me that she always destroyed my letters so that John would not find out about us. She would not have lied to me.

I raced home hoping that I would not be stopped for speeding. Luck was with me. I left the vehicle and went into the house. No one had noticed me, I hoped.

Over the years, Alicia and I had rarely talked about the day of the Forresters' murders because whenever we tried, I would choke up. Alicia's calm demeanor and her support as strong and consistent as it was, always made me wonder where that depth of strength came from.

The day after the Forresters' deaths, I understood how deep her love was for me and mine for her. We were the soulmates people write about. We did not judge one another. What was in the past would stay in the past.

It was that last Tuesday morning, after I had made breakfast for Alicia, when I heard her call. I knew something was wrong. I went into my wife's bedroom; she was half out of bed.

I rushed to her and settled her back in bed. She was frail; I knew that she knew her last day was near. As I sat by her bed, Alicia touched my arm and said, "It is too late for me."

She then reminded me of that day so long ago. Alicia told me that she knew about Marisa's pregnancy. Alicia told me that she had talked to Mae earlier that morning; Mae wanted advice about how she should tell John about the baby. Mae wanted to *tell John that the baby was mine. Alicia said that she told Mae to tell John that day, but to say it was John's baby.*

John would know soon enough and it would be best if she just confessed. If Mae told John the baby was mine, both women knew that John would come looking for me, but of course, he never did.

Then my Dearest took a last, long breath and uttered her final words: "Marisa, you have...You will not destroy my..."

I started to say, "Of course, you know that I love..."

I realized what she had said. I remembered that ghastly day when I had arrived home. Alicia had known the details about Mae's death. She said that Amanda had called her, but I realized that that had been a lie. Alicia's dying words were the last words Mae had heard before she was stabbed.

I had not seen our white car driving away from Mae's house, but Alicia had been there.

I had guessed that fact many years ago, but I kept quiet. She was faithful to me; she also knew what I had done.

At the end, I held Alicia in my arms for a long time. She has been my life and she has stood by me knowing what I had done. I have stood by her. My lust destroyed three families.

Alicia's failing health has finally set her free. She

will never have to answer for her loyalty to me. I will never have to answer for my loyalty to her.

I know that the time has come for me to answer for my sins, but I will decide how it ends.

James and Nancy, I ask you not to judge me and your mother too harshly. We loved you and wanted to protect you from the horrors of that day and what we had done. We will spend eternity suffering for what happened.

Chapter Twenty-Eight

"There you have it! So, it was Robert Evans who killed the Forresters and Amanda Griswold," Richard declared when they were finished reading.

"It may be a technical point, but the coroner at the time of Marisa's death felt that her stab wounds were so serious that she could not have survived. Even if we believe that Evans shot Marisa as he claimed in the diary, I'm not sure how we would have handled it if we hadn't gotten our hands on these journals," Susan said.

"It's a moot point; he's dead and we now know how and why it happened. We can close the cases on the Forresters' and Amanda's deaths," Karen stated.

"Green's enormous error was not checking Evans for a weapon," Susan declared, stating the obvious.

"I'm not defending Green, but he had no reason to suspect Evans; Evans had reason to be at the Forresters' home; he was delivering a package," Karen pushed.

"What puzzles me is why John Forrester was discovered by Evans to be holding the knife," Susan questioned.

"It seems to me that he could have stabbed Marisa in a fit of rage," Richard answered.

"Well, we only have Evans word that that did not really happen. John could have discovered Marisa with the knife still in her and pulled it out thinking it would help," Sarah answered.

"There are many problems with this diary. Evans said

that he was mistaken about John killing Marisa, but he said it in a sly way," Susan said.

"Didn't he say that he knew who did it?" Sarah asked.

"He did allude to that, but notice he didn't say he 'knew' who did it. They had a pact of silence for all these years," Richard asserted.

"Even after Alicia died, he could not bring himself to say that she was the one who stabbed Marisa. It does answer a question we have had since we saw the tattered hate letter," Karen reasoned.

"What are you thinking, Karen?" Susan pushed.

"Notice that Evans referred to his wife by the name of 'Alicia' in the diary, but only gave us her name as 'Arlene' in the interview," Karen answered.

"What's significant about that? I call my Aretha 'Sally,' which is her middle name," Richard retorted.

"Exactly, that is what Evans did in his diary; he called Arlene by her middle name, Alicia. I asked Sarah to check with the Florida DMV for Evan's wife's driver's license; you know the answer; her given middle name is Alicia. Even after she passed, he didn't need to pretend any more. He gave us the name of Marisa's attacker without actually saying it. He left it to us to connect the dots. I am positive that she stabbed Marisa," Karen surmised.

"That makes sense; Alicia is the one who wrote the hateful, warning letters to Marisa; signing them with her middle name," Susan added.

"Right, the mice chewed most everything in the

'signature' so it confused us."

"Arlene, Alicia, was seen leaving the Forresters' house by Griswold shortly before Evans arrived," Richard agreed.

"So the car Amanda said that she saw racing away that day was definitely Arlene's, Richard," Susan pushed.

"Evans said that Arlene knew about the Forresters when he returned home that day; she gave her husband a weak story that she had talked to Amanda that day, but he realized that her story could not explain how she knew some details of the tragedy.

"He sensed from that very day she had stabbed Marisa, but he could only admit it after Arlene died," Karen said.

"So he kept his mouth shut for all these years to protect his wife," Sarah said.

"Not only her, he was a coward who couldn't take the responsibility for what he had done, so he was not about to confess. And Arlene knew what he had done, ergo, the pact of silence," Richard declared.

"Amanda Griswold's murder was really senseless. If she had not tried to blackmail Evans about the fourth letter, she would be alive today. Evans was not going to permit her to tell us what she knew about Arlene's or his involvement in Marisa's murder. He had gotten away for all these years and no busybody was going to spoil it. His mistake was writing a note to Marisa in the Welsh language.

"I believe that we might have narrowed our sights to him, eventually, and he knew it; he couldn't face his punishment and his way out was suicide. Chief Carter told me it was a very messy one."

"Well, it appears that this ugly case is over, Karen," Susan asserted.

"This case is tragic. All these years Evans thought he was the father of Marisa's baby, but the irony is that John was the father. It is sad to speculate that none of this may have happened if DNA testing had been available back then. What a tragic waste!" Karen added.

"I'll state the obvious, Karen, none of this would have happened if Evans had kept it in his pants," Susan added.

"Susan, I can always count on you to bring things to the basics. Okay, I think that we can write up a solid report for the Chief. He will be very pleased. The two Forrester siblings will have their answer and the DA can put solved to the Amanda Griswold murder."

* * *

Later in the day, Susan stopped by Karen's office for a quick chat before leaving for the weekend.

"I know you said that you haven't talked to David about your possibly taking the FBI position, but have you given more thought to what you will do?"

"Actually, Susan, I have; I'm going to talk to David tonight about it. He will be leaving the Reservation and driving to Flagstaff for a flight to Atlanta. I think he has a stopover in Phoenix on the way."

"How do you think he will take it? I know you will be traveling much more than you do here."

"I briefly mentioned the possibility to him the other night. He said that it was my decision; he would be fine with whatever I decided. He is such a love. He's home tomorrow; we'll talk more before I decide what to do."

"Well, the best to you both. I'm headed home; see you Monday."

"See you Monday."

* * *

It had been a long tiring day. The going-away party had been a complete surprise, but as tired as he was, David couldn't refuse to attend. Co-workers had thought enough of him to put together gifts, food, and drinks to make his send-off a happy memory. This last departure from Reservation would be a surprise to Karen.

The friends and the good food and drinks made the evening pass quickly. Looking at his watch, he realized that he had long overstayed is planned trip to the airport. Taking leave of the party, he said his good-byes and gulped a last one for the road. Friends tried to stop him. But he insisted and began his journey as he edged the vehicle onto the highway to Flagstaff.

The drive would be several grueling hours at this time of night; he did not want to lose his seat on the puddle-jumper from Flagstaff to Phoenix at five in the morning. He would just have to make the drive. His wife was waiting for his return in the morning.

Several times during the drive he felt himself drifting off to sleep; the road rumble strips immediately brought him back to reality. Finally, as he reached the outskirts of Flagstaff, he turned onto the two-lane road, which would take him to the airport proper.

Suddenly, he realized that two cars were approaching; one was in his lane. He veered to the left to avoid them.

The stillness of the night was shattered by the sound of two vehicles meeting head-on at seventy miles per hour. The energy of the vehicles crashing crushed the engines into the front seats; igniting both vehicles as gasoline tanks ruptured spilling their fuel onto hot engine parts where they burned until there was no more to burn.

* * *

At eleven o'clock on Saturday morning, her landline rang.

"That's strange," Karen thought, "David would call me on my cell, not the home phone."

Answering it, Karen heard an unfamiliar voice.

"Good morning, this is Officer James Levine from the Arizona Highway Patrol. I need to speak with Ms. Hunter."

"This is she; what is this about?"

"I have some bad news; early this morning a David Robertson was in a very serious automobile accident. I am very sorry to have to tell you that he was gravely injured."

Karen lurched forward onto the sofa stifling her grief. The pain she felt was stab into her heart. She was stunned into silence.

"I'm sorry, Ms. Hunter, are you still there?" Levine asked.

Karen girded her professional strength and answered, "Yes, this is his wife. Can you tell me what happened?"

"I am sorry that it took us so long to reach you; the vehicles were badly damaged and we had to check license tags to determine the drivers. I should tell you that the other driver died. Your husband has been flown to St. Joseph's Hospital in Phoenix."

Karen felt a primal scream rising in her throat, but she willed it away.

"I can tell you that it appears your husband was not at fault. He was not the accident cause. The other driver had crossed the dividing line into your husband's lane."

Karen answered, "Yes, that would be my David; he was always a careful driver; I will fly out today."

Officer Levine could not bring himself to give further details of the accident. He knew that Karen was acting stoically but must be at the breaking point.

"Ms. Hunter, I will meet you tomorrow with more details."

"Thank you," was all that Karen could say before she hung up.

After she called David's brother, Joshua, she let the screams out. Her grief was beyond anything that she could handle; she did not want people around at her time of pain.

Karen immediately went to Chief Tate's office with the news and request for an emergency leave.

Later, she went to her office; closed the door; and reconsidered her resignation letter. She also wrote the

304

Atlanta FBI Section Chief refusing his offer. She had wanted to get away from the life's work she knew, but now her priority would be to help David become well again. Her wishes would have to wait; but not forever.

Where she would go she could not say, but she felt that for her and David it might be away, far away from Middlefield. Only time would tell when and where.

About the Author

Jon A Sanborn, writing as J A Sanborn, has written six mystery novels: *The Lost Cipher, The Orion Factor, Death Comes to Ely, The Stillwater Incident, Of Friends and Others, and Recollections – An Olio of Short Stories.*

The author holds a BS degree in chemistry and a Ph.D. in computational chemistry from the University of Massachusetts Amherst.

He is a U.S. Navy veteran who served in an antisubmarine squadron, VS-34, aboard the antisubmarine aircraft carrier, USS Essex, CVS-9, at the peak of the Cold War during the Cuban Missile Crisis in 1962.

He has had a career spanning thirty years in various management positions in high technology corporations as well as fifteen years in academic settings teaching chemistry.

After retirement, he formed Swift River Publishing to provide publishing services for his own novels, and for people who have written manuscripts and wish to have them published at modest cost.

He has had a lifetime interest in physics, chemistry, ciphers, codes, and mystery stories: fact and fiction.

He and his wife of forty-seven years live in Savannah, Georgia with a spoiled tuxedo cat.

www.ingramcontent.com/pod-product-compliance
Lightning Source LLC
Chambersburg PA
CBHW062114170626
46813CB00002B/453

* 9 7 8 0 9 9 6 8 0 8 2 7 9 *